The River's Secret

A Sophie Quinn FBI Mystery Thriller

Georgia Wagner

Publisher: Greenfield Press Ltd

Contents

Prologue

She was about to die, and yet Sophie wondered if this was what it felt like to be born. Cold. Wet. Dark. Wanting nothing more than to scream at the injustice of it all.

She churned the cold, murky bayou's nighttime waters as she struggled to keep her mouth above the waterline. Gasping for air, she fought the drag of the cold chain locked around her left ankle, gouging into her ankle. She'd been warm less than five minutes ago, before her murderer had stolen her jacket and shoved her into the Louisiana marsh's nearly stagnant river. Now the moonlit chill of the dark water and the breathless exertion of her efforts not to drown robbed her of even the chance to scream.

Flailing about, her palm slapped metal and with a sudden pull, Sophie grabbed the edge of the lonely airboat the killer had used to bring her out here and took a deep breath as she blinked the water from her eyes. Her auburn hair was plastered along with her blouse to her back. Her hair tie had come out in the struggle, and locks of rich brown clung between her shoulder blades and across her arms.

The dim red of a cigar flared over her. A shadowed figure standing in the airboat shook his head, blowing out a puff of smoke as he pulled it from his lips.

"Key?" the man asked. His voice held the graveled decay of a thousand previous cigars and the callous indifference of nearly a dozen other murders. "Find the key and one goes free." The same words he'd said before shoving them in the water. "I'm a fair man. One key. One free. And one for me."

"Please," Sophie answered, gasping, splashing about, water droplets dripping from her lips as the liquid churned under her chin. "My name is Sophie Quinn!" her voice rose in volume as her body buoyed. She struggled not to swallow the turgid liquid. There was a lot in a *name.* Empathy, for one. But this man didn't seem particularly empathic. She added, with another gasp, still kicking, still struggling, "My sister is Molly! Please! You don't have to do this." She tried to keep her voice steady, to not let in the fear or the bayou's nighttime chill, but the Cajun in her voice was creeping back. Despite years of trying to suppress it, for the stage... for a television audience, it came back in the bayou. "Please," she repeated, lowering her voice, trying to draw in the man's attention by the drop in volume.

Some killers could only do what they did because they didn't see the people they attacked as real, they didn't see them as people with names and hopes and lives of their own. Confronting him on this inconvenient fact could be the leverage she needed. She didn't expect him to let her or her sister go, but if he hesitated—if he made a mistake—she and Molly might be able to get away.

The figure replaced his cigar, folding his arms and letting the shotgun in his off-hand perch in the crook of his elbow. He didn't reply.

About to speak again, Sophie felt a jerk on her leg. The manacle bit her ankle as the chain tried to yank her underwater, and she instinctively gripped the airboat to keep from being pulled below.

Molly.

Taking a deep breath, Sophie let go of the airboat.

The water deafened her and set her long hair spiraling out again. With a couple quick strokes, Sophie put enough slack in the chain and no longer felt the pull, though, she heard the clinking rumble of it through the water. Blinking, Sophie tried to use the meager moonlight to see through the murk around her. Her eyes traced the links down to the floor of the river, where they passed through the ring of a heavy anchor, abruptly turned, and began to rise again.

On the other end was her sister, Molly, bound to the same chain by the opposite end; without enough length for both of them to reach the surface, if one of them could breathe, the other was at the bottom. They alternated, taking turns breaching the surface for another gulp of oxygen. But with each pass, the burning in Sophie's arms grew, her lungs became more desperate for the night air, and the chain binding the two sisters seemed to grow heavier.

Sophie tried to refocus, fighting the muscles seizing in her chest as fear threatened to overwhelm her, trying not to look up at her sister's kicking feet by the airboat. If she drowned—simply sank to the bottom, her lungs filled with water—then Molly would have all the time she needed. She would have slack in the chain to swim back and forth until she found the key... and her own freedom. The cigar-puffing psycho might even let Molly go without finding the key if Sophie died here and now. *'One key. One free. And one for me...'* Sophie closed her eyes.

It's odd the places your mind goes when you're about to die.

Her mind drifted. To flee the horror of the moment? The dread of death?

Her thoughts brought her to the backstage of a second-rate magician's show in Baton Rouge.

The trick with the water tank escape is to stay calm. During rehearsal, Great Gavriel's voice relaxed enough to let the Boston lilt color his words. On the far side of fifty, Sophie could still remember the way the gray-haired magician had winced, settling his hip before slapping the transparent tank. She'd been eighteen at the time. Seven years and a lifetime ago all at once.

The petulant Sophie in her memories crossed her arms. "You promised we'd practice the hypnotism act today. I think I'm getting the hang of it and you said if I mastered it, *I* could lead in the next show."

"We *are* practicing," Gavriel replied, giving the tank another knock as he flashed a fox-toothed smile. "Swimmin' drawers are in the changing room."

We are practicing, Sophie thought to herself, her mind snapping back to the present. She tilted her head back. The wizened shape of a whiskered catfish swam past, pushing an underwater wave through Sophie's hair. Sophie let her arms go adrift. She closed her eyes. She acknowledged the chain at her ankle. The struggling splash of her sister above her. The killer holding a shotgun in the airboat. Then she let all these thoughts pass.

Autohypnosis. Just a word for self-hypnosis. Most everyone has experienced it even if they don't realize it. It's that trance one enters when driving a familiar route, suddenly realizing they're parking the car without remembering how they got there. It's letting go of all the critical thoughts and letting one's subconscious and animal instinct run the show for a bit. With practice, some people can get to that place intentionally.

For a skilled hypnotist, it's a tool.

Sophie stilled her chest. Easing the hitching tension of her lungs and quieting their demanding spasms for air.

I am safe. I am calm.

Years of practice answered her demand, and Sophie felt herself slip into trance. She let the weight of the chain pull her to the bottom. Opening her eyes, she looked at the dark river bed around her without judgment. Every reed and stone, every creeping mudbug and clink of the anchor chain held in equal and absolute attention.

I am safe. I am calm. I can find a key at the bottom of a bayou.

The only sensation was the cool of the water on her skin, the pull of the nearly motionless current, and though aware her body was moving, aware her eyes were seeing, Sophie would never be able to recall the specifics. For some unknowable time, she simply *was* the bayou.

...

Bubbles rushed past Sophie's face. She blinked. Fingernails dug into her arms. Molly shook her—no—shook her *again*. An underwater shout from her sister sent a fresh stream of air past Sophie's cheeks and into her trailing hair. Molly's brown eyes were wide with panic and Sophie felt her lungs screaming with agony as she choked with the need to breathe. She must have looked like she had drowned, another moment and she would.

Something stabbed at her palm and Sophie opened her hand. Molly looked down, following her gaze.

In her hand was a small, steel key.

One key. A rush of anxious relief flowed over Sophie, and she shoved the key against Molly's stomach, giving her sister the barest second to grab it before she turned and swam for the surface. 'One key. One free. And one for me.' No time to argue. Molly had to go free. It was a big sister's job to protect her little sister. Sophie had had a good life, her dream job, a tv show. Molly still hadn't left their parent's trailer. Even at twenty-two, she simply hadn't had the chance.

With an explosive gasp, Sophie broke the surface. Her trembling arms grabbed hold of the airboat's side as her ears flooded with the night sounds of crickets and marsh critters.

"You were down a long time, cher. Little sister thought you mighta drowned." The man with the cigar adjusted the baseball cap on his head, propping his booted foot on the edge of the boat beside Sophie's hand. "You find something down there? Are you the one who goes free?"

"No!" Sophie shook her head. "I—I think Molly found it."

The man gave Sophie a long, hard stare, the burning end of his cigar twirling as he seemed to chew on the thought. As the moment stretched, Sophie felt a spike of uncertainty in her stomach. What if Molly had dropped the key? She'd been shouting, trying to rouse Sophie in her trance. What if she drowned before she could unlock herself? What if the key was a trap and it didn't actually open the locks on their ankles?

A splash erupted on the far side of the airboat. Molly.

"Wait! Wait the key is here, but it was Sophie!" her sister shouted, her palms slapping the side of the airboat.

Sophie yelled, "NO! Molly! No!" Her voice echoed off the steel side of the boat. Water sprayed from her lips, dappling the metal. She stared, finding her sister's eyes in the murk. "You found the key—good job!" Sophie said, her voice firm, cold. She tugged at her ear with one hand.

The old signal.

A joke as children. *Stop pulling my ear...* Their dad had once said, mistaking the phrase "stop pulling my nose..." when the girls had joined together in some teasing prank. And ever since, pulling the ear had meant duplicity, had meant an inside joke, had meant *keep this on the DL,* between the two sisters.

In restaurants, when on a blind date, a quick ear pull and the conversation veered. At family reunions, a quick scratch of the lobe, and one sister was duty-bound to go along with some fib.

What had started as a joke, became a sacred bond between the two sisters.

"But I—" Molly tried to protest.

"No! You found it. Don't try to save me—go!" Sophie snapped, tugging the ear again, her eyes blazing.

The man let out a loud, barking laugh. Pinching his shotgun under his elbow he clapped a hurried and enthusiastic round of applause as relief washed over Sophie, driving out a breath she hadn't realized she'd been holding.

The man pulled Molly aboard—and the younger Quinn sister looked dumbstruck, stammering, momentarily taken aback. The killer clapped her back like a coach encouraging his star player after a game. He sat her down, pulling out a towel from under the seats and laying it over Molly's shoulders.

"Ça c'est bon! You two. I had a feeling. Down in my bones, I know it. You two are special. Find the key, ha! And you found it."

The murderer cast a look over his shoulder, catching Sophie's eye. Even with her sister unchained, Sophie was still locked in place. The empty manacle wouldn't fit through the anchor's ring. Sophie swallowed, keeping her gaze on the man, her stomach turning in knots.

Without even looking, the man drew out a pair of handcuffs and smoothly locked Molly's wrist to her seat.

Sophie pounded the side of the airboat. "You said she'd go free! One key, one free!"

"But she didn't find the key, did she, cher?" The man sauntered to the side of the boat, checking his shotgun.

He lifted the barrel, sighting right between Sophie's eyes. "You find the key. I set you free. But that one—" With a grin, he nods over his shoulder to Molly, "—that one's for me."

Sophie's breath caught, her heart hammering.

"Fly free. Fly to God, little angel."

Chapter 1

Sophie tasted blood. That wasn't good. She didn't usually have to bite that hard, didn't have to fall back on biting the inside of her cheek *at all.*

When the flashbacks came, they were always unpleasant, but over the last six years, they had become a mere annoyance, a small, voiceless demon that she could banish with a moment of stillness. Biting the inside of her cheek was an emergency brake, a last resort The Great Gavriel had taught her when she began to learn self-hypnosis. A happy coincidence that it worked for her flashbacks as well.

As Sophie came back to the present, the hum of the FBI field office's air conditioner replaced the creaking of crawdads and long fluorescent lights took over for the moon from her memory. Her hair, no longer stuck to her back with marsh water, was short, cropped around the ears, and swept up and back to keep it out of her eyes, though, it clung and frizzed from Detroit's summer heat. Her slate-gray professional suit and discrete athletic shoes fit in with the broad office desk in front of her and the man hunched in the faux leather chair behind it.

"Quinn? Quinn, you still with us?"

Sophie looked up, meeting the deputy director's eyes. "Sorry, Max. I'm just... absorbing it. That's all. You were saying?" It wasn't quite seven in the morning and she hoped the hour would help excuse the distant look she must have had.

Deputy Director Maxwell Meyer dropped the file he'd been referencing on his desk, fanning up the loose ends of a dozen other documents. He ran his fingers through the few black strands willing to defend the position that Meyer still had hair.

"I'm sorry, Soph. I knew this was a bad idea before I even asked you in here. I just—after what you've done for this office—I didn't want you to find out through the grapevine is all. If you need to take some leave and process things, I understand."

"No, that's not it," Sophie protested.

"Oh, it's not, is it?" Meyer scoffed. "Listen, Soph. You're a great consultant, but there's not any one, agent, CI, or otherwise, that can take a bomb like this and keep working. I know you've tried your damnedest, but the fact is you couldn't catch RK for the last six years—"

"You think I forgot or something?" Sophie replied, trying her best to keep the edge out of her voice.

Meyer sighed, his brow beetling. "No. But if this is really him, if RK is back—"

"Then another pair of women will be dead in forty-eight hours. Then another and another. And we don't even know what made him stop last time. Maybe it was my escape, but we don't *know*. What we do know is that I've investigated him more than anyone else in the country."

"Illegally," Max shot back. "Bounty hunters and PIs, that is when you haven't tried stealing confidential documents and evidence right out from under *actual* agents."

"Which I wouldn't need to do if you let me *in* on his case. I need to be on the team hunting him."

Meyer slammed a palm on his desk, "Dammit, Quinn. That's the opposite of what you need. There's a reason we don't put people on cases they have personal history with, and with RK—"

"He killed my sister, Max," Sophie interjected. Her voice low, her tone calm. The only tell that she was upset in the slightest was the steady intentionality of her breathing, and only someone with training approaching her own would be able to pick that out.

Silence.

RK. The River Killer, that's what the press called him when the true scope of the murderer's killings started coming to light. The first time Sophie had heard the name was a day after the medical examiner had called her and her parents to identify Molly's body. That's when she learned about the eight other girls. They'd been found in pairs, a new set every two days.

Molly made nine, then he vanished. And Sophie survived... the tenth victim. The one he never claimed.

For the first week, Sophie's producers sent sympathy cards and flowers. A touching tribute was made in her absence and released in lieu of a rerun. *Mysteries and Phenomena with Sophie Quinn* would be taking a hiatus while the host and star of the show grieved her sister and recovered. The second week, she received voicemails asking when she could discuss her return to the show. During the third, she received unsubtle hints and sideways recommendations on how the best way to deal with grief was to get back to normalcy as soon as possible, how her absence was putting everyone else who worked on her show in a real bind.

'Fake it till you make it'.

'Just force yourself to smile, you'll be surprised how much better you feel'.

...A full month hadn't passed before Sophie canceled her own show.

A house with a pool. Book deals. Regular stage shows in Vegas, Broadway, and everywhere in between. She even had online classes where people could pay to watch videos of her teaching hypnotism, mentalism, and illusion acts. At twenty-five, she had everything she had ever wanted.

Everything except her sister.

She sold it all. For the first six months, she'd used that 'tv money' to hire private investigators. When they didn't get results fast enough,

Sophie began to study on her own. Her mother had always said she had a freakish memory, an *envie* for words, facts, anything other people didn't know. And with two PhDs in record-smashing time, Sophie applied to the FBI. If no one else could help her, she'd make agent and help herself.

As it turned out, having even infrequent blackouts due to intrusive, traumatic flashbacks was a deal-breaker for women approaching their thirties and trying to break into the FBI. Still. At thirty-one, she had now been a consultant long enough that Meyer had relinquished a desk for her permanent use. Consultant wasn't quite the same as *agent,* but at least they allowed her to help.

Meyer finally let out an explosive sigh. He pressed a hand to the side of his head, leaning forward on his elbow. Sophie cataloged the motion, an invisible checklist running through her mind as she took in the way his fingers pressed against his cheek and brow. Now tapping. Frustrated, but not at her.

Guilt.

"Soph," Meyer started. "You've helped a lot of people since you joined our office. I'm not questioning your competence or your dedication."

"Then what's the question, Max?" Sophie asked. It was a gamble, letting the person opposite you pick the battleground for your argument. But Meyer was off his game. If she let him define what was holding him back, she might be able to overcome his reluctance.

He paused. Glancing over Sophie's shoulder, Max stood and walked to the glass door of his office. He pulled the blinds then circled back to his desk chair like an old dog looking for a comfortable place to collapse. Steepling his hands, he said, "Quinn, I've been in this job a long time. I've seen what it does to people. If you go chasing this guy and you don't catch him; if he goes to ground again... it could destroy you."

That was it then. Sophie could have laughed. It *could* destroy her? As if the River Killer hadn't already destroyed her life that night.

Sophie drew a deep breath. She leaned forward, half standing as she splayed her palms on the director's desk. "I don't need your protection, Max." She emphasized his name. Direct, familiar. "I need your help."

Abruptly the phone on Max's desk rang. Meyer glanced at the number lighting up on the cradle's display, raising a black eyebrow. He held up a finger and picked up the phone.

"Detroit office. Meyer here."

Unsure whether to stay or go, Sophie stood behind her chair. She picked at the hem of her blazer, looking at the closed blinds over the glass door, wondering if it would even be possible to focus on another case while she knew the River Killer was active again. After all these years, he was *back.* Maybe she would quit. She still had her PI contacts and new friends she'd made in the FBI.

"You're kidding."

Turning around, Sophie found Meyer already staring at her, his jaw open and slightly askew as he mouthed his unvoiced confusion.

"Yeah. Yeah, of course. No, I understand. You're sure this is a good idea?"

A pause. A hurried grunt of farewell and Meyer dropped the handset back into its cradle, drumming his fingers across the hard plastic before gesturing towards Sophie.

"Well, Quinn, apparently, you're not the only one who doesn't care what I think." Picking up the case file from his desk, Meyer walked to the door, slapping the overstuffed manila folder against Sophie's shoulder and haphazardly dropping it into her hands. "Given you're a consultant and not technically under my office, agents on the ground in Louisiana have requested your assistance on the new RK vics. Pack your bags."

Sophie nearly dropped the case file, her nerves unsure what to do now that the fight she'd been expecting had evaporated. As Meyer popped the blinds and opened the door, he waved off Sophie's quick attempts at polite gratitude. "Yeah, yeah. Just don't forget us. I'd like you back when this is all settled. Oh, and one last thing," he added with a wry grin, "Merchant says hello."

Chapter 2

Six Years Ago

"*That* was your plan?" Sophie narrowed her eyes, a faint line of disappointment on her lips as she looked away from the shotgun leveled at her face. It took every bit of self-control to look disinterested in the weapon and disappointed in the grizzled man wielding it. But she managed.

Molly, now handcuffed to the airboat's passenger seat, opened her mouth in silent shock.

A ripple in the bayou lapped Sophie's forearms against the airboat, tugging the trailing strands of her auburn hair between her shoulder blades and the thin chain locked to her ankle. But the cigar-smoking murderer did not pull the trigger. Sophie guessed what the man expected: panicked pleas not to shoot, a hurried hand held up as if she could stop the slug destined to scatter her brains across the water. Denial. Bargaining. Anger. He'd seen those before.

But boredom?

That was the one reaction he wouldn't know what to do with. And a man as careful and methodical as this would do what any confused predator would do. He'd pause. He'd wait. He'd try and find the trap before he stepped in it.

He hesitated.

Locking eyes with the murderer, Sophie said, "Too obvious. My first guess was that you would kill us both. Saying you'll let one person go and then killing both isn't clever. It's just a common fib—are you really that insecure?"

The man's cigar flared, a sharp inhale. And a dusting of ash fell between them.

Sophie scoffed, tugging on her ear then rolling her eyes and looking past the man as if embarrassed for him. "Where did you come up with the idea? A comic book?"

"Shut up," the man demanded.

One hand holding her steady, Sophie's other hand let go of her ear, gesturing with an exaggerated twist of her wrist. He was about to snap. His tone had been easy, playful even, but now—

"No? A movie then? Don't tell me you got this from a tv show."

That did it.

Most people think you have to be calm and willing to be hypnotized. It's true, to a point. But really, hypnosis is simply opening a mind to suggestion. Reactive, not thoughtful, like dominoes falling in a chain.

In that final moment, Sophie could only hope she'd arranged these particular dominoes correctly. He'd throw the cigar, then he'd shoot.

The man reached for his cigar: a prop. It made him feel calm, in control, as much a part of his murderous character as the playful voice he affected. It was theater to him. He turned to the side to toss the stub into the water as Sophie predicted he would, his head turning ever so slightly away from the sisters.

Molly was ready.

As soon as the man turned, her one uncuffed hand flew forward, tossing the manacle key to her sister. Sophie lunged forward, snagging the key just as the murderer's cigar hit the bayou. She'd seen their secret sign, a tug on the ear, intuited Sophie's gestures.

The man cursed, twisting around and raising his shotgun. A slug blasted through the lip of the airboat's wall, but Sophie had already dropped below the surface.

She swam under the boat, hiding in the shadow. Her hands wanted to tremble, but her practiced nerves forced them still as she found the lock at her ankle.

A blast from above her, and Sophie saw the torpedoing slice of a slug shot into bayou water. She ignored it. Her read on the man was correct so far. He'd hate feeling tricked. He'd be reactive, suggestible—but would he shoot through the floor of the airboat to get her? She suppressed her uncertainty as the key struggled against the water-filled padlock, then with a forceful twist, the manacle clicked and slid off her foot.

Sophie spiraled under the boat, turning away from where the shotgun had been fired. She'd come up on the other side of the boat.

At her first stroke though, Sophie froze.

The murderer thought he was clever. But was he? Had he fired on one side to force her to surface on the other? Would he be waiting for her there?

She could also run... swim away. Go for help.

No, she thought. It wasn't an option. Not after what Molly did for her.

It's a big sister's job to protect her little sister after all.

A muted scream cut through the murk. *Molly.* Suddenly the anchor chain rattled and the heavy, hooked steel jerked up from the river-bottom with an eruption of silt.

He's leaving! The abrupt thought of what would happen if he disappeared with her sister torched what remained of Sophie's hesitation.

Swimming to the rear of the airboat, Sophie grabbed the metal cage surrounding the enormous fan that powered the craft. The engine sputtered and roared, kicking up misting droplets into Sophie's eyes as she pulled her head above water. If she could only reach Molly, Sophie could pick handcuffs. She knew the tricks of slipping bindings and the weak points that let illusionists escape chairs and caskets and bolted doors.

But Molly didn't.

Sophie pulled herself around the fan cage, one hand finding the lip of the airboat as she blinked the murk from her eyes. Molly's seat should be right there.

A rough hand snagged her by the hair, and Sophie instinctively tried to drop away, but the twisting fingers held her tight. Her scalp screamed as he held her in place by her long, brown hair like a fish on a hook.

“Shoulda swam away, cher,” the murderer snapped above the roaring fan.

With a jerk of his elbow, he smashed Sophie's forehead against the fan cage. Starbursts flashed white and red over her eyes. She couldn't tell if the wet feeling on her face was the spray from the airboat's fan or her own blood. Sophie's legs dragged out behind her as the boat started pulling ahead. They were moving again.

“I try to be fair. Try to give a little mercy. But no.” The man gave Sophie's head another calamitous shot against the airboat's steel cage. Distantly, Sophie heard Molly crying and screaming for him to stop. “No, you don't want the mercy. I guess tonight it's *two* for me. A *lagniappe* for my trouble, dealing with your nonsense.”

Sophie couldn't see much, her head was swimming and her hands were too busy trying to pry the murderer's fingers out of her hair to wipe her eyes.

But for one perfect moment, her eyes were clear. She blinked, looking straight into the forearm holding her tight. Moonlight cut through a gap in the trees, leaving the man's face shadowed by his ball cap but illuminating the inside of his arm, by the crook of his elbow.

A tattoo. Dark, geometric. Like an Escher drawing of some impossible shape that eludes comprehension. It's odd, the things one's mind will latch onto when they're about to die.

Sophie could feel her consciousness fading. One more blow and she'd be gone. The bayou whipped by under her, pulling at her limbs and clothing as the boat picked up speed.

"NO!"

Molly, still cuffed to her seat, shot out her heel. The blow connected with the back of the River Killer's knee, driving his shin into the edge of the airboat's metal lip. With a cry of pain, the murderer let go of Sophie's hair.

She had the faintest notion of the airboat pulling away before her head hit the bayou water at speed.

Sophie woke up tangled in tree roots by the river's edge, the morning light cutting at her eyes.

Alone.

***

The difference between determination and obsession is in whose blood gets spilled. The determined bleed for what they want. The obsessed make everyone else bleed.

At least, that was Sophie's take.

She'd had to get a little philosophical over the years when even the PIs she hired had accused her of being obsessed with the River Killer. However, the copper tinge of blood in Sophie's mouth welcomed her back to the present and reassured her what she was feeling was determination.

Her own blood. Another sharp bite on the inside of her cheek.

The flashbacks were definitely getting worse.

Running her fingers through her cropped hair, Sophie disentangled the phantom sensation of RK's fingers. The hum of the charter plane's engines was silent compared to the roar of the airboat and after a few moments of deep breathing, Sophie Quinn was in control of herself once again.

She had declined the FBI's offer to arrange her flight. The commercial seat they'd booked left that same morning, but Sophie's years of success brought a distaste for being crammed, six to a row, between screaming infants and men too drunk or exhausted to realize their advances were even less charming than they were original. And god forbid anyone recognize her as *the* Sophie Quinn.

At twenty-one, after her first special in Vegas, Sophie had decided to indulge in a private flight and vowed to never fly commercial again unless she had absolutely no choice. And once *Mysteries and Phenomena with Sophie Quinn* rocketed her to international fame, she never did.

Looking out her window at the winding Mississippi, Sophie could almost feel its warm currents drawing her down.

South. Back to the bayous.

Back home.

Unease twisted her stomach. She hadn't been home since Molly's death. Not really. Chasing a few leads or collaborating with local PIs and informants... but dinner with her parents? A visit to see how Mama is holding up?

Mother, she corrected herself.

She'd been told her Cajun roots were 'charming'. That she ought to lean into them. Once or twice, when her accent crept back, producers and managers had told her, 'Being true to yourself is in', 'It'll be good for the brand', or that her audience will call her 'brave' for sharing her history.

Her history.

Sophie shook her head. People always seemed to have a morbid fascination with others' *history*. No one was ever allowed to be who they wanted to be. No. Given the chance, most people loved to play the embarrassing aunt, even to perfect strangers. *Sure, he's a brilliant surgeon now, but I remember when he used to run around with his little willie out and pretend he was a firetruck. Oh, she's got her own special on the TV, but did you know she used to chase frogs out back of a trailer? Her parents still live in one, you know, a trailer. Some daughter.*

“Stop it,” Sophie told herself. This wasn't why she was flying down. There was no reason her parents even needed to know she was here. They were finally letting her in on the RK case. That was it.

The case file lay open in her lap, she flipped idly through the pages.

Nine women.

Pictures she knew so well that she could see them with her eyes closed. Eight strangers... and Molly.

Two women, a chain, and a river. That was the MO that the FBI had started with. Beyond that, predicting RK had been an exercise in futility.

Another page. Witness statements that only highlighted how little anyone knew. Lab tests looking for DNA, chemical traces; partial fingerprints tied to the victims but never the killer.

She paused on the photocopy of a drawing. *Her* drawing from six years ago. Stark geometric lines meeting at angles that would be impossible in a physical object. No fuzzy shading or hesitation in the sketch. Even without it, she could still remember the killer's tattoo.

When she reached the latest insert, a blank page stamped with yesterday's date, she paused.

Two more women would be behind the insert. New details. New statements.

And if she didn't stop it... eight more to follow.

10mm low-carbon chain. Long links, between 40 and 50mm. Never stainless steel. Signs of struggle and exhaustion. This wouldn't conclusively prove it was RK back from whatever pit he'd hidden in for the last half-decade, but if it was him—if he picked up his pattern *exactly* as he'd left off...

Sophie turned the page.

***

As the jet pulled to a stop on a lonely, private airstrip north of New Orleans, Sophie couldn't help but smile. She smoothed her slate-gray suit coat and double-checked her black, leather laptop bag, ensuring none of the case files had slipped free and hurried to the plane's exit stair.

A black, company SUV parked a respectful distance back. A tall, lithe woman in the sort of black suit and sunglasses combination that movies reserve for hired assassins leaned back against the car's hood. Her hair, pulled into a tight, professional bun, had gone gray and the Louisiana sun gave every crease around her eyes and brow an unfair scrutiny that belied her true age of fifty-four.

As Sophie cleared the rolling stair, the woman nodded her way.

"Quinn."

"Merchant," Sophie replied, her smile broadening. It had been months since she last heard from her friend.

The older woman tilted her head, giving an assessing look up and down the length of the private jet.

"You know you're not here on vacation, right?"

Sophie straightened up. "No, ma'am. I'm here to catch a murderer."

"Really? Because you're grinning. You happy to hear two women were brutally murdered, Quinn?" The tall woman, Merchant, folded her arms, her fingertips rolling impatiently across her bicep.

Sophie felt her throat tighten, feeling like the new girl in the office again.

Lidya Merchant had been her Supervising Agent the first time Sophie had consulted for the FBI and the closest thing to a friend Sophie had ever had in the Louisiana field office. The older woman was sharp and carried a brand of unapologetic confidence that made the average person anxious they were wasting her time before they even opened their mouth. She and Sophie shared certain cosmopolitan sensibilities, eclectic taste in books and films for one. Sophie, from her time as a globe-trotting performer. Merchant, from her stints with Interpol and the DGSI, working with law enforcement and intelligence agencies across international borders. Sometimes, Sophie thought of Lidya as an older sister looking out for her.

So why did she look so pissed off to see her?

"Sorry, Lidya," Sophie said, softening but not completely burying her smile. "I'm just glad to see you. It's been too long."

"Yeah. I was afraid of that." Merchant removed her sunglasses and stared into Sophie's eyes, her honey-brown irises locking on like a sharpshooter's scope. "This isn't going to be like last time, Quinn. Convince me you understand that."

Sophie blinked, recoiling at the sudden confrontation. "What?"

"You know exactly what I mean. Tell me why I'm not packing you right back on your fancy jet and shipping your ass back to Detroit."

"Hold on." Sophie held up a hand to stop the accusing rush of words. "You were the one who asked for *me*. Meyer didn't even want to let me go, and you were the one who twisted his arm."

"I needed to see you. Eye to eye. You're forgetting I've worked with you before. I know how easy you can lie through a phone, through a video call even. I want you to say it to my face."

Taking a quick, steadying breath, Sophie relaxed her jaw, fighting to keep the heat rising in her face from flaring into full-fledged anger. It was a test. It had to be. Lidya Merchant never did anything without a reason. Pettiness was beneath her. So what did she want?

Sophie had no doubt that the Supervising Agent would follow through on her threat. If she didn't pass whatever trial this was, Merchant would pack her up on the next plane to Detroit. Her investigation could be over before it even started.

A knot of fury tightened in Sophie's chest. No. They couldn't do this. They couldn't lock her out again! If they tried, she just wouldn't go. She couldn't go. *He's* back. What would they do? Arrest her? With or without the FBI, she'd find him. She'd find the River Killer even if she had to rent a boat and trawl every mile of river and marsh in Louisiana herself.

"I thought so."

Sophie snapped out of her thoughts at the Agent's comment. Merchant shook her head, hiding her look of disappointment behind her sunglasses. "Invoice me your airfare back to Detroit, Quinn. For what it's worth, it was good to see you again."

No. Sophie's mouth hung open. Her mind raced to understand what had happened. If she didn't even have Lidya on her side... and then it hit her, and she knew what Merchant wanted.

"You were right," Sophie said at last, calling out over the *clunk* of the SUV's door opening. Merchant looked at her over the hood, her expression inscrutable behind her sunglasses. Sophie licked her lips and pressed on. "When you sent me to Detroit, the first time. I was out of line, and you made the right call."

"Go on," Merchant said.

Sophie attempted to hold her friend's gaze but found it difficult as she tried to stomach the words. "I am close to this case. Too close. It's personal for me. I crossed the line. I could have cost you your job. I don't know if I ever apologized for that."

"You did."

"Well," Sophie bobbled her head awkwardly, a little thrown by the interruption, "Sorry again, anyway."

The charter jet's engines whined as the small plane taxied to the end of the runway, the breeze of the passing aircraft sending a ripple through Sophie's cropped hair and puffing at her suit coat in a way that felt like a pat on the back and a soft farewell. *Alright, kid. Looks like you got things from here. I've gotta get on to New York. See you soon.*

Taking a deep breath, Sophie nodded to herself. "This case—RK—it's always going to be personal for me. But I'm ready to be part of the team. I can follow orders... ma'am."

That was what she wanted to know, right? The line between asset and liability was thin but dangerous, and Lidya needed to know which one Sophie was.

The determined bleed for what they want. The obsessed make everyone else bleed.

Merchant paused for a second, then two more. She answered Sophie's nod with one of her own, then climbed into the SUV and closed the door behind her.

A moment later, the passenger door opened.

"I hope for both our sakes you mean it. There are people who didn't want you pulled in on this. We're *both* going to be watched. You screw up this time and we're not talking reassignment to Detroit. It'll be an arrest warrant. You understand?"

"Yes, ma'am," Sophie answered.

With a final shake of her head, Merchant beckoned after her. "Get in. We're meeting your partner at the Medical Examiner's."

"Partner?" Sophie asked, buckling in. "I thought we'd be working together again."

Pulling out of the airfield and back onto the highway, Merchant replied, "Like I said, we're both under the microscope this time. I'll be supervising, but the higher-ups wanted someone impartial partnered up with you."

"A babysitter?" Sophie asked.

Merchant let out a sharp exhale, "Think of him more as 'judge, jury, and executioner'."

Chapter 3

"Of course she's supposed to be here. She's with me, isn't she?" The agitation in Merchant's voice caused Sophie to flinch in spite of herself. The young woman behind the coroner's office front desk, however, simply popped a fresh bubble in her chewing gum as she gave a disinterested shrug.

"She's not on my list and doesn't have ID. Did you get her cleared? Access to evidence is restricted for CIs and Consultants without Hitchens' sign off."

"He did sign off. I got the go-ahead this morning."

"And yet," the desk clerk clicked her tongue and pointed her pen at Sophie, "she's not on my list."

Merchant's jaw popped with restrained anger, and she nodded towards the desk. "We're meeting Agent Greer and the Medical Examiner, and you have a whole stack of temporary IDs right there."

She wasn't wrong. Sophie could see the stack of passes laying out in plain view between them, waiting to be activated for just these sorts of occasions. They even seemed to match the format she'd seen when Merchant flashed her ID to the clerk.

The drive in from the airfield filled Sophie with nervous energy. She knew from the dossier she'd been given that they'd be a ways north along the Mississippi, but as the drive progressed, as she started to see where specifically they'd be, creeping familiarity started chittering out of every dogwood and hickory. Rural. Out of the way from Baton Rouge but not quite kissing the state line.

Home.

Her old mentor didn't pry into Sophie's personal life, and she appreciated her for it, but the proximity of her folks' trailer park, good old Beech Run in the town of Peillon, no doubt compounded the anxious aura around her. If she noticed, the older agent didn't say.

Instead, Merchant had warned Sophie the field office down here was a special brand of strict ever since her dramatic departure for Detroit. Still, she hadn't expected to see the red tape so quickly. The supervising agent's caution that some folk down here didn't want Sophie involved came back to mind, and Sophie wondered how much of this was purely bureaucratic. She was already going up against a killer who had evaded capture for over six years, could she really go up against the agents she was supposed to be helping as well?

Merchant's jaw clicked again, and Sophie could sense their collective blood pressure rising.

"Wait," Sophie interjected, drawing the clerk's attention before Merchant's anger bled into her words. It wasn't much of a plan, but weighed against the idea of waiting another hour or even a half-hour while Merchant procured her an official ID, well, it was worth the risk.

"Here it is. Sorry, boss. First day nerves," Sophie said this last bit to the desk clerk as she reached into her bag, ignoring Merchant's confused stare and pulling out a slim wallet. Fumbling her wallet, Sophie let out a squeak as it slapped onto the desk.

In response, the clerk rolled her eyes and her turquoise earrings betrayed the subtle shake of her head as she seemed to silently say, *Lord, if these two don't get their act together and get away from my desk—*

"Sorry, sorry." Sophie scooped her wallet back up and turned it over hurriedly, showing a white plastic ID badge with VISITOR stamped across it in tight, blocky lettering, safely tucked behind the plastic fold where a driver's license would usually go.

The young clerk blinked, looking into the open wallet. Sophie slapped it shut, sliding past the desk apologetically and hurriedly saying, "Thank you so much. Appreciate your help."

Merchant followed her away from the confused young woman guarding the entryway, waiting to speak until they had rounded a corner.

"I thought we agreed to play this by the book," Merchant growled.

"And I thought you had permission to bring me in on this case," Sophie rebutted.

"I do. Look, just keep the magic tricks to a minimum, alright?"

Sophie nodded, turning over the pilfered ID card she'd slipped from the clerk's desk and making it dance between her palm and fingertips, disappearing and reappearing, as they crossed into the examination room.

Metal cadaver drawers lined the walls and a pair of sterile, metal carts in the center of the room held various autopsy tools at the ready. Two bodies covered in white sheets lay on a pair of larger carts in the center of the room, ready for any further examination the ME cared to give them.

Merchant's breath fogged in the temperature-controlled air as she sighed, "Looks like we beat Greer here." Quickly glancing to the discrete blue-steel watch on her wrist, she added, "I'm going to track down the ME and get this business with your ID sorted before Hitchens throws a hissy-fit over it."

Merchant snatched the twirling card from between Sophie's knuckles, pointing it at her. "Stay put and try not to get yourself in trouble. Can you do that for me?"

There was no time for a reply, as Merchant already had her cell phone to her ear and stormed out into the hallway, leaving Sophie behind.

Alone. With two bodies.

Sophie was by no means squeamish and her consulting position put her in contact with more corpses than the average celebrity magician, at least, she hoped it did. But there was something about the cold, dead silence of the room that made sitting still impossible.

Within a minute, Sophie had circled the exam room, looking at the tools, the open documents and lab results spread across wall-facing countertops. Against the Louisiana heat, her suit coat had been sweltering, and she'd left it in the car. But in the strict chill of the autopsy room, she started to miss it. Could she pop out to grab her jacket? No, until Merchant sorted this mess out with her ID, she'd better not risk it.

A pale green surgical gown hung by the entrance, and Sophie was tugging at the warm-looking fabric wistfully when the door flew open and a man in a tan suit ran her over.

Sophie's arms wheeled as she tried to catch herself, the fluorescents overhead coming fully into view and her shoulders making a beeline for the tile floor.

The man's eyes went wide, and the styrofoam cup in his hand dropped out of his grip. Lunging forward, one hand catching her by the elbow, the other catching her by the waist, he gave Sophie the split second she needed to pin her heel to the floor and steady herself.

Glancing from her to the freshly spilled coffee on the exam room floor, the man visibly winced.

"I'm so sorry," he said, gently letting go of her and quickly grabbing a roll of maliciously thin, brown paper towels from the counter. "Stupid of me, I know. And it looks like I didn't even need to rush." Sopping up the drink and condensing the used paper towels into the now-empty cup, the man tossed the whole mess into a nearby basket marked 'Hazardous Material'.

The man seemed capable of carrying on the conversation on his own, so Sophie let him. Taking a step back, she got a good look at him. He was tall, probably a good inch or two over six feet, putting him half a foot taller than her, and his tan suit hung on him neatly, not loose or with the pinched folds of a suit too small to accommodate its inhabitant. But the suit wasn't new either, she could see the wear at the sleeves and the hem of each pant leg. It was well cared for nonetheless, and given how well it fit and how many years he must have had it, Sophie gathered that there was a fair amount of trim muscle beneath that suit.

"I'm meeting Agent Merchant and a new consultant," the man said, wiping off his hands on the last scrap of paper towel. "But it seems I beat them here. You must be the new ME, Ms. Walsh, right?"

When he stood up and met her look, Sophie was struck by the clear, crystal blue of his eyes. He had to be a decade older than her, the gray starting to salt his hair, and the small creases at his lips and eyes put him in his early forties, but an active forty. The sort that could round up eleven other guys and rob a casino.

He extended a hand along with the question and an earnest look begging her to forget that he trampled her less than two minutes before. A part of her wanted to be mad but soon gave up. With a sigh, she shook his hand and replied, "You must be Agent Greer."

He smiled. “That I am. A pleasure to meet you.” He motioned back towards the surgical gown hanging by the door. “I assume you were getting ready to leave, and I don't want to take any more of your time than we have to.” Sweeping the gesture back to the two covered bodies, he continued, “So what do we know?”

Sophie blinked. “Oh, wait, I think you—“

Agent Greer checked the time on his phone, “I don't know where this consultant is, but I'm sure Agent Merchant will understand if we start without her. Not sure how much she'd comprehend anyway.”

Stiffening a bit, Sophie held back her intended comment, instead asking, “Why do you say that?”

Greer shook his head. “I only found out she was being called in this morning, but no one would tell me *why* she was being called in. I guess some people had bad experiences with her back a couple years?” He shrugged. “Wasn't here back then. I'd never heard of her, but my daughter recognized the name. Says she has a podcast... or something, I don't know. I just know how these departmental favors go sometimes, and I hope this isn't a babysitting job for some snooty internet-celebrity type.”

Sophie bristled as the man crossed the room. “You think they'd waste resources bringing in someone who couldn't help?” There hadn't been anything malicious in Greer's tone, if anything, he simply sounded... tired. Resigned, perhaps.

He let out a soft chuckle. "Maybe not. But do I think Hitchens would try to buy a cheap favor bringing in a celebrity on a case he doesn't believe will get solved? That, that I'd buy."

Looking up, Greer now saw Sophie standing with arms folded, one raised eyebrow unabashed in its criticism. He scratched his neck, looking towards the bodies once again. "Apologies. I'm just... tired. Haven't had my coffee yet," he looked wistfully towards the Hazardous Materials bin. "Just tell me what you've found out and I'll get out of your hair."

Sophie chewed her lip. She glanced between the files she'd been skimming and the sheets over the bodies. The cautious part of her told her to correct Greer's assumption before this went any further. Another, louder, part of her said to show him how much she could *comprehend*.

"Fine. You're familiar with the River Killer?"

Greer nodded, "Got the file this morning, I'm up to speed."

Sophie scoffed under her breath and drew back the sheet on the two bodies. She'd seen the preliminary reports, so she was ready and took grim satisfaction in Agent Greer's breathy murmur of 'Jesus Christ'.

"They were found overnight," Sophie explained. "Conditions show they've been in the water less than a day, but as you can see, we're guessing an alligator got to them by the serrated nature of the wounds."

"River Killer couldn't have mutilated them?"

Sophie shook her head. "RK doesn't use blades. Gators—Alligators," she corrected herself with a slight cough, "they won't eat a person in one go. If they can, they drag the body off to store it. Push it up under a log on the river bottom." She pointed to a series of bruises on the throats, first on one victim then the other. "The chains around the victims' throats are the likely cause of death, but also the reason the alligators didn't drag them off. They were chained neck and chest to a tree."

Why would he do that? A sense of disquiet settled over her. Sophie hadn't considered the point until that moment, but her thoughts quickly retraced the original nine victims from six years ago. They'd been left out on the edges of rivers, just like these two women. But he hadn't chained them in place. Why? Why this particular change in the formula?

"It's a declaration," Sophie said softly.

"A declaration of what?" Greer prompted.

"He wanted to make sure they didn't slip away. He wanted us to find them." Sophie's brow furrowed in thought. "He plays games. That's what he does. He sets up challenges his victims can't possibly win. He sees himself as clever. *Needs* to be seen as clever. It's maybe the most important part to him. He wants an audience."

"Is he?" Greer asked, his own features now drawn in focus.

"What?"

"Clever. Is he?" he repeated.

For a moment, Sophie was beneath the airboat again. Indecision. Fear. A fatal guessing game of what he knew and what he intended. "I don't know," she said at last.

At that moment, a dark shape caught her eye, and Sophie leaned down, examining the first woman's wrist. Hurrying around the table she turned the second woman's arms, then her legs.

"What is it?" Greer asked, quickly following her to the cart's edge.

"Tattoos." Sophie pointed to the dark, floral pattern riding up the second woman's ankle. "They both have tattoos."

"Is that significant? Hold on, we have a sketch of RK's tattoo in the file." Before Greer could pull up his phone, Sophie shook her head.

"No. This is wrong." Sophie's stomach fell. "Six years ago, during the original investigation, the FBI fed the media a false tip. They said all his victims had tattoos. A public lie. It's a tactic to weed out false leads, but sometimes it draws the killers in. Serial killers hate to be misunderstood."

Greer let out an appreciative whistle. "That's smart. Don't imagine you learned that in med school?"

Sophie barely registered the remark, replying almost automatically, "I have a double PhD. One's in criminology."

Greer seemed taken aback by that, scratching at his clean-shaven chin, he tried to meet her eyes. "What's the other in?"

"Not important right now." She felt like the room was spinning. What did it mean? Why would RK go out of his way to imitate a false lead? Was this part of his game now? He wasn't just toying with the victims, but with the FBI.

It's not about the FBI. It's about you. You didn't die, so he's not done playing...

"Ok," Greer said, "Maybe it's a coincidence? There are lots of women in Louisiana with tattoos. If he really doesn't care, then maybe we shouldn't either. Chalk it up to happenstance."

"No," Sophie said. "No such thing. Not with him."

The door swung open. Greer abruptly turned.

"Boss, you're going to want to hear this. Ms. Walsh—apologies," he held up a placating palm to Sophie, "Dr. Walsh has a theory about these tattoos and—"

A woman in blue scrubs embroidered with the name 'Walsh' stopped short in the doorway. Merchant, stepping past Greer, held out a fresh ID card.

"I'd love to hear this theory, Quinn. But why don't we start with why Agent Greer believes you're the coroner."

Chapter 4

He took a deep breath. The smell of brick dust and stagnant canalways filled his lungs with explosive desire.

Almost good enough to overshadow the irksome, squawking laugh of the gaggle of young people up the road. He frowned. There was a time they would have had their laughs in the local drug store, sipping a shake from the bar or taking a glass bottle of soda to walk with. There was a solidity to that idea.

But not anymore.

Styrofoam cups. Aluminum cans filled with god-knows-what, shipped in from god-knows-where.

Nothing solid. Nothing rooted.

Just like them. So rootless and oblivious that they had no idea the man had been following them for the last hour.

The murderer guarded his eyes from the flare of mid-morning sun shooting between uneven rooftops by pulling his baseball cap down until it was almost a mask. He didn't need to see the high-fronted shops along the old town's mainstreet to picture them. He could imagine the wrought-iron window rails and balconies that led off old apartments on second and third stories of the buildings crowded shoulder-to-shoulder down the thoroughfare. Most of them were only storage attics now, but that didn't erase their history. History was important after all. Learning, honoring, those who came before you.

History. It was baked into the cobblestone of the street under his feet. Seared into the ugly patches of asphalt that filled cracks and gaps the small town didn't deem worthy of authentic restoration or even routine maintenance.

An old pickup gave a clipped honk behind him, and the man skipped up onto the sidewalk. The street wasn't crowded, but there were enough people that the man didn't have to perform this ritual alone. As expected, there wasn't anywhere else to be on a Saturday morning in Peillon. As he passed, murderer and truck driver shared friendly waves. Civil reassurances. *No harm, no foul, friend.*

One of the youths, a young man in a letterman jacket, backdated three years by the patch on the front, let out a braying laugh, shoving his skinnier companion into the street in an act of horseplay. The curtain-haired brunette in a summertime top and jean shorts laughed along while her older friend, hair a touch shorter but just as brown, pointed at the pickup and gave a panicked shout.

The truck swerved around the roughhousing boys, giving a quick blast on the horn that elicited a wave of middle-fingered salutes and an attack in the form of a mochaccino grenade lobbed woefully off-target.

The acid-brown coffee hit the street and began to seep between the cobbles as the now-empty cup rolled into a storm drain.

The murderer nearly stumbled. Indignation burning in his chest. *Soon enough, mon petit. Soon enough.*

The offense was soon forgotten though. The two young men wrapped their arms around their dates, urging them across the street to the Lime Tree Cinema for a matinee.

It was with some interest that the murderer noted how the young man in the letterman jacket, *Mason Guidry*, tried to lean in for a kiss with the short-haired girl, *Brooklyn Cortia,* only for Brooklyn to demure, looking up the street after the pickup truck's taillights and accepting Mason's kiss with disinterested patience on her cheek.

The foursome disappeared into the shadow of the movie theater lobby, and the murderer pulled a small notebook from the pocket of his jeans, brushing the hem of the thin, gray overshirt that covered his arms to the wrists. It sweltered in the summer heat, but for his purposes, it was a worthwhile sacrifice. He couldn't be too careful.

He flipped a few pages ahead, glancing up just to be sure the group hadn't changed their minds and left the Lime Tree. He knew they wouldn't. Three Saturdays in a row, they hadn't. But again, he couldn't be too careful.

Under 'Brooklyn Cortia + Mason Guidry', the murderer added another line. Everything counted, no matter how minute. In a way, it *was* like theatre. They had a part to play, just like *he* had a part to play. But before the show, the audition. He had to be sure they were right for the role. Had to understand how they fit the grand scheme of things.

Other kids their age were off at college or taken up with a trade. Brooklyn had a job at the diner several doors back, and Mason fashioned himself a handyman, riding around with his pop and doing just enough to not get swatted. The murderer thought about that kiss again and wondered if losing Brooklyn would change the boy's perspective on things. Not that it mattered to him much. It was mainly the idea that appealed to the murderer. One little thing. One person snuffed out.

He knew personally how much that could change someone.

The Lime Tree Cinema smelled like stale popcorn, and there were runs and old burn marks in the lobby's concrete-flat carpet. It had two screens, Right and Left. The numbers had long ago fallen off.

He didn't need to check his notes. Just as he expected, Mason was carrying his usual tub of glistening popcorn. Brooklyn had a small packet of licorice and soda.

The man grinned and bought a matinee ticket for Right.

Walking past them, he settled into his seat, he liked to sit close to the front. He would see who came and went without being obvious. People were nervous about others sitting behind them, but in front? No, no one would give a damn.

And just like before, it was only him and them in the theater. The four in their own little world, a world that did not include him.

He waited an hour, checking his wristwatch. The movie was the same awful schlock that each generation's young people ate up. Scantily clad women. Reckless boozing. Heroic violence. When the hour had just about passed, he stood and retreated to the hallway.

His heart beat faster. *Patience. Soon enough.*

Under his sleeves, he felt the coil of nylon rope wrapped close to his forearm. Discrete. Strong.

He slipped the end between his fingers, a noose sized for a throat. Ready. A knife in the other hand, softly clicking open and closed. Open. Closed.

He thought about the van, parked in the theater's alleyway more than an hour before. The chains in the windowless back.

Enter stage left. Brooklyn Cortia, an empty soda cup in her hand, walking for the theater bathroom. Seeing him walking towards her. Looking away.

Their shoulders nearly touch.

The murderer's hand flies up. Brooklyn flinches.

His hand covers his mouth for a rough cough. A murmur. "Sorry, cher."

She ducks into the bathroom as he crosses to the alleyway door.

He checks the time again. A nearly perfect rehearsal.

Now, onto the show.

Chapter 5

There had to be a better word than awkward, Sophie suspected. Thanksgiving dinner with relatives you barely know is awkward. Your show's guest getting sloshed before performing in front of a live audience is awkward.

Getting sent out to investigate a lead with a man you met moments before after tricking him into thinking you were an FBI medical exa miner... that had to warrant a new expression.

"So..." Sophie tested, "Do you at least want to listen to some music if we're not going to talk?"

The agent in the tan suit gave a perfunctory grunt and gestured to the radio without removing his thumbs from the wheel.

Sophie sighed.

Greer's face had been a mask since they left the coroner's office. He had his guard up. Sophie could see it in the precise way he kept his hands at ten-and-two and the tight set in his jaw. He rapped his fingertips across the leather steering wheel and subtly bobbed his head in a way that said, *I'm mad, but calm. I'm not going to make a big deal out of it.*

I could open him up, Sophie thought. Cars were a great place for hypnosis. The steady rhythm of the road. The focused point of attention that kept the conscious mind occupied but left the subconscious free. If she just started talking, started shaping that subconscious, she could have him apologizing to her inside ten minutes.

No.

She decided immediately that was a bad idea. She'd already broken his trust, and if Greer was specifically chosen to be her babysitter during this investigation, there was a chance he would be ready for any type of manipulation. Hypnosis is a somewhat delicate technique, sometimes all it takes to stop it is the conscious thought of 'I don't want to be hypnotized'.

Sophie settled back into her seat, noting the unusual cleanliness of the cupholders and floormats around her.

Unlike Merchant's monstrous SUV, Greer's sedan fit the bill for discrete and low-profile. The only possible exception to this was the solid white body. But then again, this wasn't Chicago or New York. Down south, white cars are common, and as they silently clipped along the highway, Sophie noted to herself that the only other place she saw half as many white cars was California.

Merchant handed off the reins to Agent Greer outside the coroner's office. Walsh, the actual medical examiner, had little to add beyond the highlights Sophie had already addressed, and with the sun about to hit its mid-day zenith, the supervising agent gave her final orders to the newly minted partners.

Deciding she'd had enough of the silent treatment, Sophie broached the only topic she was sure Greer wouldn't ignore.

"So, this bed and breakfast, the, uh," Sophie checked the case file, "The Cotton House. They said the vics, Demi Wilson and Hazel Michel, were cousins. Do you buy it?"

Greer gave her a funny look. "Why would they lie about that?"

Honestly, Sophie didn't believe it either, but at least he was talking. If her involvement in this case came down to Greer's good will, she had some serious ingratiating to do.

"All of RK's other victims were either related or longtime friends," Sophie explained. "But this detail with the tattoos, it's itching at me. I don't have a grip on it yet, but I feel like something's different this time. RK is changing, evolving maybe. Making us second guess our assumptions."

"What difference does it make? Cousins, sisters, best friends; RK killed in pairs but they didn't all have to be blood relatives. They just had to be—close."

Greer was right. Sophie and her sister hadn't been the only relatives targeted in the River Killer's original spree.

The GPS on the agent's phone beeped as Greer pulled into a gravel parking lot.

"This is the place," Greer said pocketing his cell phone.

A wrought-iron sign highlighted in chipped, white paint proclaimed 'The Cotton House' like an enormous set of braces hanging free from their teeth. The broad, two-story house had a classic Southern charm to its wide front porch and broad open windows facing into a dining room.

Three other cars were politely spaced beside a weedy garden and a drainage ditch: two commuter four-doors and a pickup piled up with dirt-encrusted landscaping tools.

As they pulled to a stop, Sophie pointed to one of the cars, a light gray sedan with Arkansas license plates. "That's them," she said.

Greer gave a brief grunt of agreement and they walked over to the car together.

"Locked," Greer said, checking the latch.

"I see bags." Sophie put her face to the passenger window. "Looks like spare clothes and some camping supplies."

"They didn't even unpack?" Greer tilted his head, chewing on the thought.

"Might have just been passing through. It's not the smartest thing, but I can imagine not wanting to unload everything for a night's stay only to have to load it all the next morning."

"So what then? RK just happened to be here and just happened to pick this one night to abduct them?"

Sophie shook her head. "RK's meticulous. He doesn't do 'spur of the moment'. If he took them, he had a plan in place. He might not have even taken them from here. We're right on the edge of Peillon. They could have walked into town. If they paid cash, they may have even had dinner or hit a bar. He could have taken them anywhere along that line."

"If it's even RK," Greer added, scratching at his neck.

"It's him," Sophie shot back.

Greer shrugged. "You're the consultant."

At first, Sophie wasn't sure why the comment stung her, but she felt a small flush in her neck and cheeks at Agent Greer's open skepticism. In the coroner's office, he'd been an enthusiastic supporter of her theories. Now he seemed to hold every comment she made at arm's length. She'd have to show him. She knew she was right.

Leaving the car, the pair marched to the front door. A large, wooden porch swing hung by twin steel chains. Sophie's photographic mind automatically logged them. *6 mm links. Stainless steel.* Too thin, and not the right kind for RK's purposes.

The doorbell buzzed and the sound of chimes from inside the house returned to them through the open front window.

A short man in a blue button-up shirt and dark suspenders answered the door. His shoes were scuffed but looked as if they'd once been quite nice, authentic leather too, judging by the cracks shot through them. Bulldog jowls added an undertow to the wobble in his red-brown beard as he swung his chin to face Sophie and then Greer, a smile as cracked as his shoes greeting them.

"Welcome to the Cotton House. Yes, we have rooms available and there's a discount if you're willing to pay cash."

Greer drew out his ID. "We're actually here about an investigation. Are you—"

The door swung shut so quickly that Sophie barely registered the abrupt darkening in the man's expression. She flinched backward as Greer's foot shot into the jamb, catching the door before it could latch.

"No! Absolutely not. I do not consent to this unlawful entry."

"Sir," Sophie said, intentionally keeping her voice low and calm. "We're here about two of your guests, not you or your establishment. We called ahead. Your employee confirmed they checked in last night."

The man, who was giving short, pointed kicks to the tip of Greer's shoe, trying to dislodge it, raised an eyebrow and huffed.

"Don't know anything about that! I'm sorry, but my customers' privacy is sacred, and if you think you can come in here and start tearing up the place like it's some—some—*crack house*, well, you've got another think coming. This is still America and I have my rights."

Greer's own expression darkened now. Leaning forward, he spoke in a soft, steady rhythm, like loading a revolver. "Listen. We want to do this the nice way, but if you want to do it the hard way, we can. I can get a warrant, a K-9 unit, a whole SWAT team down here to tear up every bit of rotten drywall, every floorboard you got—"

"Then do it," the bulldog-chinned man snapped. "Go on. Get your warrant. I'll wait. It'll give me some time to tell the eleven o'clock news how an honest businessman is getting abused by the—"

Sophie had heard enough. She took two quick steps to the side, reaching the porch swing she noted earlier. With a quick push, she set it swinging then turned to face the men in the doorway. She drew her shoulders back, lifting her chin as she softly cleared her throat.

Both men looked her way. The soft creaking of the porch swing behind her added a beat to the background hum of cars passing on the highway, like a metronome.

"Mr. Brand..." Sophie started. "Richard," she continued with a gentle smile. The softness in her face was organized precisely for sympathy without blame. Apology without guilt. "We're not going to do anything you don't want. We won't touch a thing. Won't go anywhere you don't approve." He wanted to argue, she could sense it, but the ticking rhythm of the porch swing subconsciously told him to wait. "Two women are dead. Demi Wilson and Hazel Michel. They were cousins. We don't believe you had anything to do with it. In fact, I don't believe anyone who has stayed at your hotel had anything to do with it. If we look at their room though, we might get an idea of who did. The trail leads us to your door, but it doesn't end there. Will you let us pass through?"

Without really intending to, Sophie's voice drifted back towards her stage persona. The tone and cadence could easily have been between her and an audience volunteer on *Mysteries and Phenomena with Sophie Quinn.*

Greer seemed enthralled, no longer looking at the small man in the doorway but piercing her with those sapphire blue eyes of his. Not hypnotized himself, he'd not been the mark, but with a focus as if he might be trying to hypnotize her back. Almost.

Sophie snapped her finger behind her back. Softly. So quiet Brand might not have consciously heard it. The proprietor took a quick breath, the exact sort one takes when startled out of a dream.

Richard Brand, the Cotton House owner, sighed. Chewing the inside of his lip, he gave a disgruntled shake of his shoulders. "Fine," he said. "Just—don't bother the other guests, would you? Times are hard enough as it is. I don't need you scaring away my business."

He pulled away from the door, leaving it ajar for the pair to follow. Greer pushed it open and gestured for Sophie to enter first. He was still staring at her, and Sophie felt her stomach tighten.

Does he know what I just did? He didn't seem to know anything about me in the coroner's, but what if that stunt just jogged his memory? Sophie wasn't sure what the legal ramifications of hypnotizing someone to gain entry to their business were, but she had a feeling the straight-laced agent in the tan suit behind her would go out of his way to find out.

Mr. Brand left them at the end of the downstairs hallway. A bedroom door with a copper-plated 4 on it marked the guest room. As he left, he gave a final look over his shoulder, his voice half a cough. "All I know is that they checked in last night. I gave them their room key and they went to bed. I haven't seen them and assumed they were just tired, as they didn't come to the table for breakfast. It's only just noon after all. I didn't even know they were gone, till I heard about your call."

Sophie gave the man an understanding nod, and with that, they were alone with Demi and Hazel's room.

Two narrow beds flanked the room, the sheets disheveled and unmade. Rustic décor of pastoral paintings and a taxidermied duck filled the space around a wood-burned plaque that pictured a grill fork and the stylized question: 'what's for dinner?'

The room didn't smell musty, per se. Just *close*. And the ceiling fan kicked on with a hum along with the light switch. With the motion of the air, an acrid, chemical smell rushed up to meet them.

Greer wrinkled his nose in distaste.

"Chloroform," they both said, nearly at the same moment.

Sophie stepped to a pair of totes at the heads of the beds. "Looks like a change of clothes. Some toiletries. Just like we thought, they only expected to stay the night."

Greer, nodded as he pulled open a chest of drawers. "Nothing in here." Dropping to his hands and knees, the big agent took a look under the beds. "So. Hypnotist. I'm starting to remember now. You had a show, right? Is that what you did with Brand out there?"

Biting her lip, Sophie looked for anything else of interest in the cramped room. This was it. After tricking him and now seeing her hypnotize a potential witness, his next call would be to Merchant, or maybe this 'Hitchens' guy, and she'd be off the case.

"I'm sorry about that," Sophie answered. "I don't go around hypnotizing people on a whim. I promise. We just... needed to get in, and it didn't look like he was going to budge, and—"

"No, no," Greer reached under the bed. "You did the right thing. The guy was a brick wall. But we're in and nobody got hurt. Victimless crime as far as I'm concerned, Miss Quinn."

That surprised her. Sophie spun to face him as the tall agent pulled a pair of purses from under the bed. She wasn't in trouble? From his tone, it even sounded like Jonathan Greer approved of the stunt. Sophie smoothed her suit coat. Maybe she'd misjudged him. Maybe there was a chance this partnership might work out after all.

"If anything," Greer continued, smoothing the bed sheets and turning out the purses, "I'm shocked it actually worked. I always thought that was a carnival trick. A con that used an audience plant, that sort of thing." Lip gloss, tissues, a few spare tampons, and even a set of pliers spilled out on the bed among a dozen other odds and ends as Greer set to sorting the items for anything strange.

"Some acts are," Sophie admitted. "It takes effort, sensitivity, to make the real deal work. A lot of people get impatient or don't have the touch for it."

"Sensitivity? Like what, a psychic?"

"No. Nothing like that. I just mean being able to read someone. To tell what they're thinking or what they're about to do from body language or verbal cues. Their tone and the like." Sophie walked the room again.

She paused by the window. Her eyes on the dirt path behind the old house-turned-hotel. The room was stuffy, but women traveling alone, staying on the ground floor of a hotel wouldn't open the window at night.

Yet she felt a breeze.

Sophie inspected the latch. The metal was scraped, gleaming bright scratches in the otherwise dull metal. The wood also looked gouged in places.

Sophie pulled the metal lever back and pushed the window. It slid open cleanly and silently. Everything else in the hotel squeaked and groaned, but this one window opened like it was brand new.

"Jonathan, come look at this," Sophie said over her shoulder.

Greer approached, saying patiently, "I'd appreciate it if we kept it Agent Greer, Miss Quinn."

Sophie closed the window, then pulled the latch's brass lever back in place.

Locked.

She looked Greer in the eyes, then pushed up on the window. It slid open once more, just as silent as before.

Greer whistled. "He broke the lock while they were asleep and crept in?"

Sophie shook her head. "No. See the metal seams have been cleaned and oiled. He knew they were going to be here. He *knew* they would stay in this room. He prepared the window and broke the latch, leaving it looking like it still worked, but removing the pin under the lever. He was ready for them that night."

The unease rolled off Greer as he bent and inspected the windowsill.

"How though? They just got into town."

"I'll bet you anything," Sophie answered, "If we look at their social media, the girls posted their plans for the trip. Or asked for advice on where to stay locally. It doesn't take much."

Abruptly, Greer's attention snapped to the dirt alleyway behind the hotel room window. He turned on his heel, rushing for the door of the room, and Sophie bolted after him. "What? What is it?" she asked.

"Tire tread," Greer answered gruffly.

The pair raced around the side of the hotel, running to the back. A dirt alleyway between a copse of trees and the drainage ditch, just wide enough for a car to pull through. Greer held up a hand, keeping Sophie back. His cellphone camera snapping away, he gestured at the faint tire marks in the dirt.

"One set of treads," he said quickly. "No one else has been through."

Sophie tried to see what he was seeing, but the weave of the multiple tires made it difficult for her to tell how many cars had passed. "How can you tell?" she questioned.

"I was a military engineer, Marines. Between the contractors and the enemy, I've seen just about every vehicle used for just about anything. It was, well, a unique education."

Sophie could see it now. The agent's quick reflexes, the speed with which he moved from relaxed and affable to stern and focused, his physical fitness. He was ex-military.

"This is it. This is our lead." Greer smiled at the pictures he'd taken on his phone, then turned, looking at the row of windows along the back of the hotel.

"There." Sophie pointed out the victims' room.

"Perfect." Greer indicated a deep groove in the dirt, then four other points that he also photographed. "The van was parked right outside their window. Just ahead, so the back doors could be open without blocking the window itself."

"Hold on. Van? What van?" Sophie tried to follow the Agent's rapid gestures, but he soon rushed back to his white sedan.

When Sophie caught up, she found him opening his laptop.

“The kidnapper used a van. A big one, like a work van. Maybe an old Dodge or a Ford by the wheelbase. The turn radius at the corner shows she's a beast.”

Sophie thought about the marks she saw in the dirt. She supposed it was plausible, but the speed at which Greer recognized and put it all together was still astounding to her.

Greer's fingers ran across the laptop keyboard, rattling the hood of the car from the aggressive typing. “By the wear in the tread, I'm guessing she's old. Different designs and levels of wear too. He's had to replace those tires, but not recently.”

Suddenly Sophie saw where he was going with all of this. “So if you cross-reference old work vans in the area with criminal records—“

A final, solid snap of the Enter key, and Greer spun the laptop to face her.

“And we get one Victor Holland. Assault and battery. Harassment. And the proud owner of one 1998 Dodge Ram van.”

Chapter 6

Anxiety and nervous clenching started to ball up Sophie's stomach the way it always did when she thought of home. Beech Run trailer park was on the other side of town, along with her parents. So, in theory, she was safe. In fact, the last time Sophie had been in Peillon, the Magnolia Arches trailer park hadn't existed.

Magnolia Arches had neither magnolia trees nor any triumphant archways. Though, judging by the painted sign beside the squat office building near the entrance, they at least tried to preserve the memory of the triplet of white-bloomed magnolias that used to stand there.

The memory was old, but Sophie could imagine before the ground was flattened and covered in crushed rock. There must have been some pecan trees here too. About the only thing that could get a small, barefoot Sophie Quinn away from frog racing on the creeks and scaring her friends with lies about which logs were actually gators was the prospect of a pocket full of pilfered pecans.

Greer slowed down their sedan as they crossed the gravel-covered bridge over the roadside ditch that separated the trailer park from the main road, and the jostling motion drew a quick breath from Sophie as she refocused on her laptop.

"We should be careful," she said. "Victor missed his last meeting with his parole officer."

Greer rapped a finger on the steering wheel. "You think he's running already?"

Sophie thought about it. If this were any other case, she might say yes. Alternately, she might even suspect that they'd find Victor Holland on a bender in his trailer. But if this really was RK...

Staring into the man's mugshot, Sophie tried to reconcile the image with eyes that haunted her dreams, shadowed and lit from below by a smoldering cigar like the fires of hell itself. Would they find a tattoo on Victor's arm? His rap-sheet didn't indicate one, but Sophie had seen more grievous oversights from small-town cops.

"No," Sophie replied. "He's not running. He just started again. He thinks he's safe. I wouldn't be surprised if he opens the door to talk to us. His ego has probably convinced him that he can talk his way out of any suspicions that come his way." A bitter bite crept into Sophie's tone. "We should be careful because if he really is RK and he's missed that parole meeting, he did it on purpose. Whatever game he's playing with us, part of it may include luring cops to his home."

Greer glanced her way, not taking his eye off the narrow gravel avenues between the trailers for even a full second. Out of the corner of her eye, Sophie could see the appraising way he weighed her words, but he didn't reply.

"Here we are." The tall agent clicked his tongue and pointed through the windshield.

Sophie froze. Not because of the trailer Greer pointed out, but because of the home two lots down from it.

Bright pink so textured that it seemed to breathe. Patchy attempts at repainting mingled with age and the oddities of trying to match the unusual color. Begonias and baby's-breath in pots that barely obscured the coffee cans the flowers had been started in. And a rain-smoothed statue of a chubby angel leaned over in prayer, its elbows propped on a stone etched with a mix of letters and numbers that Sophie knew all too well.

After all, it was 2 Chronicles 7:14, her mother's favorite Bible verse.

"Oh, come on," Sophie muttered under her breath.

"What? Did you see him?" Greer leaned forward, hustling the sedan into an open spot in front of the trailer between Sophie's parents' and Victor's.

As Greer scoped out Victor's trailer, Sophie turned the other way. No lights on that she could see. The old station wagon wasn't parked outside either.

They're not here. Sophie let out a sigh of relief. Then, turning back to face her partner, she found herself face to face with Greer's piercing blues, one eyebrow raised.

"Whose place is that?" he asked. No subtlety or attempts at offering her an out.

Sophie could feel herself starting to blush. She absolutely did not want to get into her family history with a man she just met. Besides, her parents weren't home, so there wouldn't be any need.

"No one," Sophie said, opening the car door and rounding the sedan.

Greer joined her, quickly catching up as they started towards Victor's home, a much more sedate blue that, while chipped around the edges, was at least consistent in its coloring.

"You know, not once in all the times I've heard the words has the answer 'no one' actually been the truth."

"Has the real answer ever turned out to be your business?" Sophie knew she should be more diplomatic but keeping her voice at conversational volume was the best she could manage.

Greer took two quick steps and turned, his broad-shouldered frame now a wall blocking her path.

Feeling the anger starting to boil in her, Sophie's gut reaction was to keep walking and drive a knee straight into the obstinate man's groin. The restraint not to was mainly drawn from the recent revelation that Agent Greer was formerly US Marine Greer, and while she didn't imagine the man would hurt her, the result would undoubtedly be embarrassing for everyone involved.

"What?" Sophie demanded.

Greer's face was stone. The relaxed, even excited, camaraderie that she'd experienced when the pair had explored Demi Wilson and Hazel Michel's room at the Cotton House had vanished. Sophie braced herself. This was a face she'd seen before on a dozen other men over the years. Her producer had the same expression when she'd told him she wouldn't be coming back.

Here it comes, Sophie thought. *The speech. Straighten up and fly right because it's my way or the highway, little lady.*

But, as if he could hear her thoughts, Greer's expression softened. His blue eyes drooped just a little as he said. "Look, I can tell being paired up with me isn't exactly your cup of tea. Some of that's probably my own damn fault. We didn't exactly set each other up for the best first impressions."

Sophie's neck stiffened, her eyes narrowing. Was the big man trying to apologize? Sophie could see in the agitated motion of Greer's fingers and the way his eyes kept trailing from her back to the mid-day sky over Magnolia Arches that he was uncomfortable. But by the focus in those eyes as they returned to her moment after moment, something else was happening here.

"What I'm trying to say," Greer said, plowing along with the words despite his discomfort, "is that I'm sorry if I've made you uncomfortable or given you reason to feel we're not on the same team here. I'm going to do the best I can to keep you in the loop. I realize now how much this case means to you."

So that's it. Sophie felt her jaw clench. Either when he was updating the case notes back at the Cotton House or on the drive over, Jonathan Greer finally put together that Sophie wasn't just some celebrity consultant they pulled for the case. She *was* the case. Victim number ten. The one who got away and sister to victim number nine, Molly Quinn.

Greer must have seen Sophie's growing agitation, because he gave an almost imperceptible nod and his voice dropped slightly as he added, "I think you deserve to be on this case. And I promise, I won't keep anything from you. Can I ask for the same?"

Sophie swallowed. The agent's body language said he was earnest. His mixture of anxiety, focus, and the sudden stillness of expectation was the exact same shared by gamblers all over the world. That posture when the dice have flown from the hand and all that's left is to see if lady luck will smile on you.

If Sophie had detected an ounce of manipulation in the man, she would have told him exactly where he could stick this particular olive branch.

But she didn't.

"That pink trailer back there," she jerked a thumb, gesturing over her shoulder. "That's my parents'. They didn't live here before, and I wasn't expecting to see them."

"Do you want to drop by?"

Sophie started. She squinted up at the tall agent. How could the same man be so insightful and so clueless at the same time?

"No. Actually, I'd prefer it if we got this done quickly. I haven't seen them in six years. Not since my sister's funeral."

Greer nodded sympathetically. Sophie shook her head, tossing back her head the same way she would when her hair had reached the small of her back. Now the close-cropped strands only tickled along the backs of her ears. She knew it was a transparent attempt at nonchalance, but there had been too much new information in the last day and her reserves of self-control were already running light.

"Ok," the big man said. "Doesn't look like they're home anyway. We'll keep this brief."

The pair reached Victor Holland's trailer and gave the plastic frame of the screen door a quick rap. After a count of three, Greer moved the screen and hit the wooden door with an accompanying shout of "Victor Holland."

By the dark edges around the blinds, Sophie already suspected the trailer was empty. The silence that answered them only confirmed it. But they couldn't leave. Two women were found last night. By tomorrow night there'd be two more. Unless they found him and stopped him. Merchant's warning to behave herself briefly returned to mind.

But there was simply no time.

Sophie stepped off the porch step. "I'll go left. You go right. We'll see if there are any open windows or an open backdoor."

Greer didn't protest. Chewing his lip, the blue-eyed agent simply nodded and strolled off to the right, giving the nearest window an appraising poke. Sophie did the same, quickly disappearing around the left side of the building.

Once she was out of sight, Sophie opened her coat, reaching into the inner pocket and sorting through a few 'essentials' that she always kept on her. A clasped pocketwatch on a brass chain. Cliche, but when it came to hypnotism sometimes expectations worked in the hypnotist's favor. A deck of cards and a black permanent marker she would fiddle with or use for autographs when paper was in short supply. A pack of gum. Fingernail clips. And, neatly folded in a small, black, leather clutch, a set of quality, steel lockpicks.

She waited another two-count, giving Greer time to move along the side of the trailer, then turned back, heading towards the front door, her lockpicks discretely palmed—

And nearly ran into Greer, already standing at the front door.

Startled, Sophie secreted the lockpicks up her sleeve. Had he suspected what she was going to do? Turned back to catch her breaking protocol and breaking into the suspect's trailer? The anxiety of being outwitted by the former marine quickly dissipated as he met her gaze with an equally surprised expression.

One hand on the door handle, Sophie saw Greer's other hand slip something thin and metallic into the pocket of his tan suitpants.

“That was fast,” Greer said, then with a cough, he gestured to the now-open door. “It, uh, turns out it was unlocked. And—“

Sophie let out a quick, bright laugh. She waved a hand, cutting off any further comments from Greer.

“It's ok, Agent Greer. I believe you.” She shook her head with another, now almost silent, chuckle. “Now let’s get in before—“

A loud voice shouted, “Hey! You!” as a sharp bang cut her off.

Chapter 7

A second bang, the clap of metal and plastic locking together, sent Sophie's stomach into her shoes. Part of her wished the man shouting at her was holding a gun instead of a disposable tin serving platter. At least then she would know exactly what to do and how to react. But the clatter wasn't gunshots, it was the slamming of car doors on an old station wagon parked outside a bright pink trailer and the jostling of metal trays piled too high for stability.

So, instead, all Sophie could do was step down from Victor Holland's porch as she held up a palm and tentatively called back, "Hi, Daddy."

The man stopped short, the myriad shakers of seasoning piled precariously on his serving platter fell together with a rattle, and he shifted his elbow to keep from losing the tray entirely as his large, brown eyes nearly goggled out of his head. He was wearing a rough set of jeans, work boots as calloused and scraped as his knuckles, and a loose, short-sleeved button-up over a dark t-shirt emblazoned with a cracked and faded logo of the University of Louisiana football team, somewhat stretched to accompany a torso that hadn't decided if it was a barrel chest or a potbelly.

"Sophie?" the man said so softly it could have been a prayer. "Sophie! Zadie! Zadie come here, our little girl is back."

Sophie gave a pained smile that echoed the genuine article spreading on her father's face. Like a puppy too excited for rational decisions, her father took one step towards her then remembered the tray in his hands and doubled back to set it on the hood of his car.

A large woman appeared at his side, a sweet summer smile on her lips and a floral bandanna tied around her hair. The embroidery on her blouse showed signs of fraying but was bright and clean as the day it came off the rack. Even her flats looked so clean that they almost seemed to magically repel the dust and gravel with every step.

"Sophie, oh *mon petite*, you should have let me know you were visiting. Come here." The large woman, Zadie, crossed the gravel lot as Sophie took a few more steps forward, stranding Greer by the dark opening into Holland's trailer. "Oh, baby girl, ça va?"

"I'm fine, Mama," Sophie replied as her mother closed the gap and wrapped her arms around her in a tight hug that included a delighted little shimmy and a kiss on the cheek.

This was not the time. Sophie felt her heart rate climbing, the muscles in her cheeks trending towards a frown. "Listen, Mama. I'm glad to see you too, but—"

Zadie moved her palms to Sophie's shoulder, holding her like she was a balloon that might float away. Over her shoulder she called, "Noah, stop fussin' with all that and come hug your daughter!"

"Mama, I can't—"

"I can't leave it in the car," her father, Noah, called back. "I'll be right there."

Sophie's jaw clenched; she fought the urge to shout over her parents. They had no time. Victor Holland could be back any minute and if there was evidence in his trailer—

"You haven't seen her in ten years, you old fool. 'Sides, they won't be here for another ten minutes," Zadie rebutted, muttering a hushed *couyon* under her breath. Then turning to her daughter with a smile, she said, "We're having a crawdad boil with some of the church folk, but there's plenty for all." Gripping Sophie's hands in hers, Zadie shook them and emphasized, "Plenty for all."

Ignoring the desire to correct her mother's hyperbole and reinforce that it had only been six years and not ten, Sophie tried to pull back her hands. "Mama, we're not here for a party. We—"

"We?" Zadie gasped, finally releasing one hand to cover her mouth, while she gave a wide-eyed look over to Greer, who left Victor Holland's dark trailer door to stand beside Sophie. "Oh my Lord! Noah! Noah, set that pot down this instant, your daughter's back and brought home a new beau, and a handsome one at that."

Sophie nearly choked. Ripping her other hand from her mother's grip, she let out a furious growl. "I'm not here to see you!"

The words cut like a whip crack and all at once, the animation and commotion of Zadie's chatter and Noah's haphazard unloading of the car stopped. Her cheeks hot with frustration and embarrassment, Sophie's voice continued to climb. "This isn't a visit. It's just bad luck. I'm looking for Victor Holland, and the fact that you're here instead isn't a happy coincidence, it's an inconvenience and a distraction. As usual. Now, please, just leave me alone."

Sophie's mother drew back. Her arms wrapped around her waist as if her ample body was trying to coil into itself like a hermit crab into its shell. Her lip trembled and with the immediate glimmer of tears rising in the woman's eyes, it wouldn't take someone with Sophie's skills to read the damage the words had done.

Sophie bit her lip. She didn't know what else she would have said. It was all too raw. Even six years later, it was like a bleeding wound to her. Molly was dead. Her killer was on the loose—is killing still—and they're boiling up a barrel of crawdads with the church like nothing was wrong.

A metal snap resounded, and at first, Sophie thought that her father had flung down the pot and serving trays he'd been unloading, but she quickly realized the sound had come from behind her.

"Shit!" Greer swore.

A man in grungy jeans and work boots darted from the open trailer, the metal and plastic of the screen door slapping back into place behind him. With Sophie and Greer both clear, Victor Holland sprinted for the gravel alleyway between trailer lots.

Like a shot, Agent Greer was after the man. Sophie hesitated only the briefest moment, her eyes darting towards her parents, taking in the hurt and confusion writ large on their faces. A part of her wanted to apologize, but she knew she wouldn't find the words fast enough. Her own pain would have to suffice.

Sophie's photographic memory only needed a moment, the blink of an eye, and the image was etched into her mind more exactly than any camera or transcript.

Then she ran.

Victor Holland was bare-chested, seemingly only partially dressed when Sophie's outburst convinced him to flee. Lanky and lean, with a body used to outdoor work, he dashed ahead. His tangled, brown hair, while not overly long, flipped and flared with every sharp turn as they pursued him between the haphazardly placed mobile homes.

Sophie was fit, but not long-legged like her tan-suited partner. Instead of trying to get ahead, she merely ran to keep up, throwing her gaze around the lot and trying to think ahead of their fleeing suspect.

Her eyes lighted on a concrete slope, and the sight of the sun-dappled waterway linked up with her childhood memories of Peillon.

"He's heading for the canalways," Sophie called ahead.

Greer didn't answer. They were closing in on Victor, and the strong-limbed agent lowered his head as he put on a final burst of speed.

Victor sprinted for the lip of the canalway. A stone hump, like a street curb, and a smooth granite slope that slipped five feet or so into a stretch of lazy bayou water forty feet wide. He didn't cut his pace or make any adjustments to the right or the left. He couldn't jump it. Did he think he'd lose them if he swam to the other side?

Then Sophie heard it. An airboat, a lone fisherman finished for the morning, cutting up the canalway at a leisurely pace. Not too fast for a desperate man to make a diving leap—just like hopping a passing freight car at a railway stop.

"Greer! The boat!" Sophie shouted, pointing ahead.

Too late. Victor leapt from the concrete slope for the boat. The tired fisherman at the helm let out a squawk of surprise as he was knocked clear, hitting the murky water with a splash. Greer jumped just as Victor gunned the engine, one hand slapping the metal hull as the airboat kicked up a surge of water, speeding away.

Sophie grit her teeth. No. He couldn't get away. Turning from the canal, Sophie quickly assessed the trailer homes around her. Car. Car. Motorbike. Empty trailer. *There!*

Holding her breath, Sophie rushed to a jet ski, tied to a small trailer with bungee cables. The towing-trailer itself was unattached, and with her heart hammering in her chest, Sophie checked the seat's storage bucket.

Keys.

Sophie kicked the blocks from behind the trailer wheels and rolled the jet ski to the edge of the canal. Victor had reached a bend in the waterway, and the wake of his stolen airboat was the only track Sophie could now see. The engine roared to life, and mounting the newly freed water vehicle, Sophie took a steadying breath and shoved back against the floor of the trailer.

Rattling and scraping the whole way, Sophie fought to keep the jet ski upright as it rode the concrete into the canalway with a tremendous splash. Barely missing Greer as he helped the fisherman out of the water.

Sophie slapped the seat behind her. "Get on."

No time for questions. No time for argument or scrutiny.

With the tall, former Marine riding behind her. Sophie gunned the jet ski, breaking for the end of the canalway and after Victor Holland.

The concrete sides gave way to sand and earth. creeks and streams joined and filtered out. Some large. Some small. Other canalways from other neighborhoods crossed to join the flow.

"My phone's dead," Greer called out over the engine and ripping water, showing her the waterlogged cellphone. "I can't pull up a map or get backup."

"We don't need it," Sophie shouted back.

"He could have gone a hundred ways, we'll never find him like this."

"I know where he's gone."

Sophie could feel his surprise by the sudden shift in her partner's posture behind her. "What? How?"

"He doesn't know we don't have backup," Sophie replied, taking the jet ski nearly sideways in a sharp, cutting turn, threading a narrow choke into a fresh set of tree-lined waterways. "He'll assume we're beating the bush for him around here. We were at his home. He can't stay here. Can't stay in the state even. He's trying to link up with the Mississippi."

"Once he's on the main river, he could get anywhere, we'll never find him." Greer shot back.

"Not if I beat him there."

Sophie's mind churned with a flood of memories. Childhood paths, catching frogs and racing homemade rafts. Her sister, Molly, and her, friends she hadn't seen in decades taking weekend trips to isolated lagoons. Ponds really, but they called them lagoons. Her inner eye flashed with photographic snapshots of shortcuts and byways long unused. Cold, clinical memories of paper maps charted and organized by search patterns and grids, stuck with thumbtacks where bodies had been found. Countless hours and days searching the small, unused waterways for any sign of the River Killer. All of it turned to one purpose.

To beat Victor Holland to the Mississippi.

Intersecting riverways met ahead. She could see the broad, flat glimmer of the mighty river. Greer called out, but Sophie paid no mind.

She could already hear the approaching airboat. She didn't need to see it.

And as their two paths merged, the jet ski slammed into the airboat's side, Victor Holland letting out a shocked scream as Greer leapt from his seat, the momentum catapulting him into the smaller man and dragging them both to the muddy shore.

Chapter 8

The silence boiling off Victor Holland's sullen figure suited Sophie just fine. After the chase through the streams and canalways of Peillon, she could use a moment to catch her breath. He would talk soon enough. She was sure of that.

Besides, if she tried to engage with the older workman now, she was likely to lose her temper.

Agent Greer and the suspect were both covered in large swathes of dark mud from the collision as well as the subsequent scuffle that ended in Holland's hands being cuffed behind his back. However, despite the copious covering, there was one patch of skin on Victor Holland's arm that had remained uncovered.

One patch far up the forearm, near the elbow, that drove all desire to speak with the man out of her.

Because where a tattoo, dark and inscrutably geometric, should have lain, the weather-tanned hide showed only hair and veins.

Laser tattoo removal existed, Sophie reminded herself. If it was done right, it wouldn't even leave a scar. There was a chance, no matter how small, that the River Killer had gone to the trouble of having his tattoos erased. Was that why he had selected two victims with tattoos? Was that the message he was trying to send? That he remembered the trick they'd tried to pull in the first investigation and now he'd trick them with new clues and red herrings about tattoos?

By the end of the short boat ride, Sophie still didn't have an answer.

"Sit down," Agent Greer stiffly ordered.

They had left the jet ski and the airboat grounded on the side of the canalway where their owners would hopefully retrieve them and had taken Victor back to his trailer home.

Now, in his own sorely under-cleaned kitchen space, Victor was struggling to find a comfortable position with his hands still linked behind his back.

Sophie's parents had seen their return but didn't dare approach. The large pot was heating up over a fire pit behind their home and several others had joined the growing party. It was clear from the space being vacated in the abutting grass that many more were expected. Adults and children alike set out folding tables with paper tablecloths, and trays of food covered in aluminum foil and tupperware found their way to the longest of these.

Sophie closed the door, popping on the room's light as the afternoon sun began to rob the windows of natural illumination.

“Victor Holland,” Greer began. “Assault and battery. Harassment. And most recently, parole violator. You have something you’d like to tell us about, Victor?”

Keeping up the silent treatment, Victor twisted his head to the side, staring intently into the hinge of his refrigerator rather than meeting the investigator’s eyes.

Sophie knew this posture. Victor was shut down. His body hunched. His eyes distant. This wasn’t the posture of a conman trying to figure out how to manipulate the situation. It was more like a boxer who’s taken one too many shots. His gloves were up, all defense with no desire to fight back. Sophie scanned him, reading his body language, trying to shove aside her own frustration at the lack of a tattoo.

She needed his guard down.

“Victor,” Sophie said, “I think there’s been a misunderstanding here.”

Greer raised an eyebrow, but Sophie only gave him a quick shake of her head.

Victor glanced her way, briefly. A reflex, as if unsure he’d heard her right.

“Did you think we were here about your parole?” Sophie tested.

Victor looked down again. His jaw shifted slightly, grinding his teeth in frustration.

"No," Sophie continued. "Of course not. You'd been to several parole meetings already. You weren't about to bail on them for no reason. You thought we were somebody else. Not feds... not even cops."

Victor took a deep breath, chewing his lip. Everything in his posture and body language screamed uncertainty to Sophie. He made several false starts. Sharp breaths and small tensing movements in the arms and legs that usually indicate someone's about to speak, but no words followed. Greer made a similar motion, and Sophie made a quick cutting motion with her hand to stop him from interrupting the pregnant silence.

A moment later, Victor spoke.

"Thought they sent you here to break my knees. Cops don't pick locks. You weren't in uniforms neither." He gestured with his chin to Greer's mud-covered suit. "I... I owe some money. Just thought this was about that is all."

Greer's mouth drew into a skeptical line. "You thought we were a couple leg-breakers here about a debt?"

Victor nodded. "Listen, I don't want to get in any more trouble than I already am. I'm sorry I missed my parole meeting. I've been, ya see, I—" The man suddenly seemed to struggle, reaching for the right words as if his brain was in a fog.

"It's ok," Sophie said. She pulled a folding chair and sat down at the kitchen table opposite Victor, lowering her head so that she was slightly closer to the table than him, making it easy for him to make eye contact without having to look up at her. "Take your time. We're just trying to get at the truth here."

If this man was the River Killer, he was also a world-class actor. The speed and authenticity of his movements were striking, and as Sophie watched, he shook his head as if trying to rouse the energy to continue the conversation.

"I've been picking up extra work where I can," Victor continued. "Odd jobs. I'm trying to stay afloat. Trying to keep what's mine. It's hard. I'm tired a lot. That's what happened is all."

"You missed your parole meeting because you were tired?" Greer asked, the words stretched with open doubt.

Victor shuddered as he nodded. "I've just been so messed up, you know? Howard, he manages the grocery in town, he lets me come in late some nights and stock. He's a good guy. Pays me straight up. Under the table, you know? And that's important for a guy like me, you see—"

Sophie waved a hand, drawing Victor back to the moment.

"It's ok, I believe you," Sophie said. And she did. Victor was rambling. His mind was in free flow, but she didn't believe he was making it up. "Mr. Holland, we're not here about your debt or about your parole."

Blinking, Victor asked, "Then why are you here?"

"We're here because two young women were murdered last night," said Sophie. "We're here because certain evidence says you may have been the man to do it."

Victor's leg shot out. The table shook and his chair flew into the wall behind him with a sharp crack. "I'm being set up!" he shouted. Greer stepped forward, trying to get ahold of the handcuffed man, but he twisted like a snake, suddenly alert once again. "This is a frame-up! I didn't kill anybody. You can't say I did."

With a sudden leap forward, Victor Holland overturned the table, shouldering into Sophie and trying to make a no-handed dash for the doorway. Thrown back against the refrigerator, Sophie felt her head crack against the hard plastic and let out a hiss against the pain.

In that brief instant it took for her to wince, Sophie heard the sharp report of two blows connecting. And when she opened her eyes again, she saw Greer holding a slumping and dazed Victor by the elbow. With grim determination, the tall agent walked their suspect to his overturned chair, set it up, and shoved him down into his seat again.

His voice was smooth, confident, but with a grain that showed the capacity for command and volume being held at bay, and perhaps the tattered fringe of a long-kicked cigarette habit. "Mr. Holland, if we have the wrong man here, then I sympathize with your situation. I truly do. But regardless of what you did or did not do, if you do not keep your conduct civil, then this interview is going to continue in a much darker room and under much less comfortable circumstances." The edge in Greer's voice was impossible to miss, and Sophie found herself quavering, just a little, as the final syllable passed. "Now," he continued. "Apologize to Miss Quinn and let us finish this interview, so we can all get into some fresh, dry clothes, all right?"

Gulping and offering a hurried nod, Victor said, "Sorry, Miss Quinn. I'm just—I get so riled up sometimes. But believe me, I did not do this. I did *not.*"

Righting the table and folding her hands at her waist, Sophie let her features fall into the very model of control. "Two women were murdered, taken from their rooms at the Cotton House last night. What do you have to say to that?"

"Last night?" Victor interjected. "It couldn't have been me then. Like I said, I stock overnights for Howard sometimes. He'll tell you. I was there, last night. Hell, they probably have me on the loading dock camera grabbing palettes."

"What time?" Sophie asked. They didn't have a clear time frame for when the women were taken from their room, but even with a boat at hand, he would have needed hours to take them out, kill them, and leave the bodies before they were found in the pre-dawn dim.

"I go in after all the regulars have been let off. After my regular work too. Eleven o'clock. It was a big shipment too. I don't think I got out of there until close to four or so in the morning. The cameras will show, I'm sure of it."

Sophie's stomach sank. It wasn't *impossible*, but as her eyes flitted to the man's bare arm, her intuition told her the story would check out. Victor Holland wasn't their man. They needed a new angle.

And at that, the door to the trailer home rattled with a sharp series of knocks.

"It's them," Victor moaned, his eyes wide as he looked from Greer to Sophie. "You gotta protect me. Please!"

Snap!

Chapter 9

Three perfect dress rehearsals. The murderer snapped his pocket notebook shut and took a deeply satisfied breath. The electric tension running through his limbs was delicious, and he couldn't help but hum as he stepped between the bright limbed ash trees. Even the crunch of the woodland detritus under his feet and evening birdsong lifted his spirit.

Yes, three perfect dress rehearsals, but they were nothing to the success of the first performance.

He was certain the cops would recognize his handiwork. He had been precise, exacting in his preparation and execution. They had to see it for what it was. Yes... Unless the local PD buried their head in the sand, he had no doubt the FBI would be arriving any day now.

The murderer traced a calloused finger across the bark of a gnarled hickory tree, feeling the strength of it as he crossed under the limbs. It's solidity.

For years, his heart had felt heavy. The burden of not living to one's full potential was a ponderous weight. It robbed him of sleep and every step felt as though his shoes were filled with lead. But now... the murderer's humming descended into a throaty chuckle, a secret joke shared between him and the evening's setting sun.

The snap of a branch broke his reverie, and the murderer froze.

He had walked this old trail dozens of times. No one should be here. Not for another hour.

His van was parked beside the trail's entrance into the narrow passage through the trees. He could still see it and the poorly kept, dirt parking lot that held the trail's only signage beside a pair of rotted picnic tables.

"Hello?" he called out, adjusting his ballcap to better see between the shaded trunks.

No answer.

Stage fright, he told himself. The success had filled his body with nervous energy and he needed to release it. If he didn't, he'd be jumping at shadows. Yes, stage fright, that's all it was.

Even now, despite days and days of rehearsal, he had still come out to double-check that the tree he'd selected had not changed. The day of his second performance and he was still checking the props and scenery.

Well, better safe than sorry, he supposed.

Tromping back to his van, the murderer checked his gloved hands, making sure the leather grip was tight. He checked his belt and found the bowie knife secure and ready.

The van used no fancy electronics. No keyfobs or other digital glitz. No. A metal key was better. More solid.

He shivered at the satisfying *snickt* and *ca-chuk* of the key unlocking the van's back doors and pulled them open.

With one arm on each door handle, the murderer didn't have a hand free to defend himself when a sneakered foot shot out from the back of the van and struck him in the chest.

He stumbled back with a groan, hot red flashing in his eyes. No! This wasn't right. Not how it was supposed to go!

The lanky, young man in the back of the van gave a muffled scream from behind the duct tape sealing his lips. His hands were still bound behind his back, but the zip-tie intended to bind his ankles hung over one sneakered heel, the other foot clad in only a sock. The little sneak had somehow worked a shoe off and freed his feet.

Scooting forward, the young man tried to shoulder his way past the murderer and out of the van. He was as tall as the man and in the prime of his life, but the lad had always been gangly, and despite his best efforts, his hands were still bound behind his back.

The murderer snatched the young man by the throat and growled, "Wrong. Wrong, wrong, wrong!" With each snarled 'wrong' the murderer thrust the young man's head against the edge of the open car door.

He collapsed, a thin rivulet of fresh red staining the van and dripping onto the leaves and twigs underfoot.

Veins stood out on the murderer's brow, his lips quivered, and his hands trembled. He could still salvage this. It wasn't all ruined. He could make this work. He just needed to be fast. Damn it! Why did he make him do that? This wasn't the way it was supposed to go.

Reaching into the van, the murderer grabbed a coil of strong rope. The knot reassured him. He'd practiced it hundreds of times with a mannequin. Dressing the plastic feet in boots, sneakers, flip flops, any shoe he could find. He had prepared and rehearsed, and the knot came together in a flash of hissing rope.

Dragging the young man by the tied rope around his feet, the murderer took a steadying breath.

He hasn't lost too much blood. It will still work. He can still make it work.

The show must go on.

Chapter 10

By Sophie's reckoning, there weren't many things blessed about small towns. But even she had to make an exception when within a half hour of her call, the local PD had verified Victor Holland's claim. The grocery manager, Howard, had verified his account, and formal copies of the store's security footage were being made for her case records.

And over the next few hours, Sophie felt the thrill and tension of their investigation slowly unspooling into a large, looming question mark. Their one suspect cleared, they were back to square one, with only the question of where to look next and who to talk with.

Despite Victor's initial fear that the knocking at his trailer door was his loan shark come to collect his kneecaps, the visitor had turned out to be Sophie's father, Noah.

"What are you doing here? We're conducting an interview with a murder suspect?" she'd hissed through the screen.

In answer, the heavy-set man had offered a set of fresh towels and said, "Your mother and I noticed Victor and your partner there was soaked through and then some." Then, calling over Sophie's shoulder, he added, "They may hang a bit loose on ya, but if you want to get outta those wet clothes before you prune, I'm happy to loan you some things."

Despite Sophie's frustrations, she wasn't about to force her partner to stay soaked through the rest of the afternoon. She thought again of the way Greer had thrown himself into the canal in their initial chase to catch Victor. There was a determination in the man that Sophie found herself admiring, a focus that she wasn't unfamiliar with herself.

After the local PD cleared Victor, the pair crossed to the party, which had overflowed from Noah and Zadie Quinn's lot into the grass commons of the park and the lower ground that touched the canalway waters and creek runs.

As they walked, Noah gestured at the various cookpots over gas burners and fire pits and the assorted tin trays and open tupperware. The crawdad boil was piping along, and a heavy, brown gumbo let out an aromatic sigh as the round, metal lid was lifted by a heavy woman in a flowery summer dress and bare feet ladling out portions into children's waiting bowls.

"Now you help yourselves," Noah said firmly, "It's past lunch and headed toward supper and if I know my daughter, you ain't had nothing yet today. Am I wrong?" He waggled an eyebrow and chuckled at his own comment.

"We're really not here to visit," Sophie said softly, trying hard to keep her emotions in check.

"I know," Noah replied, his smile fading, "You've said as much already."

Sophie blinked and looked away. She felt her face starting to burn and tongued at her teeth while she tried to avoid Greer's look. This was exactly why she didn't want to run into her parents. Obligation. Expectation. Why was it so difficult when they'd made it abundantly clear they didn't want anything from her?

They still had Molly back then, Sophie thought grimly. *Now I'm all they have, and the black sheep is better than no flock at all.*

Zadie sat in a reclining chair by the front door of the pink trailer, a few peeled mudbug shells lay on the paper plate beside her as she laughed along with some of the other church ladies resting in their own lawn chairs. She gave Sophie and her husband a hurried smile, before turning her eye to Greer's soaked and mud-covered suit.

"Oh, good! Noah found you," Sophie's mother said, rising from her seat. "Is Victor in trouble? When you went dashing off with him, we didn't expect to see you again, and we were all worried to bits. Oh, Lord, but look at you."

Greer answered with a polite grin of his own, gesturing with his waterlogged cellphone. "Apologies, ma'am. As far as we're concerned, no, Victor's not in any trouble. He'll have a bit to discuss with the local PD, but nothing for you to worry yourselves about."

The seated women leaned together, exchanging a few hushed words, and Sophie found herself clenching her jaw. Greer hadn't given them much, but no doubt the rumor mill would already be in full production for the next few days. She may have said something, but Zadie's cheerful voice blew through her thoughts and pulled her attention back.

"Thank heavens," she said. Then noticing the dripping cellphone, Zadie gestured towards the door. "Alright, you get yourself some dry clothes and Noah get a baggie of dry rice, let's see if we can't get that phone of his set to right too. Well, go on, dear go on. Don't worry, we won't let Sophie drive off without you."

Greer cast Sophie one last skeptical look, but with a soft shake of her head and a flip of her wrist, she muttered, "Go on. I'm going to ask around a bit. We need to decide our next step anyway."

Once Greer and her father had entered the trailer, Sophie turned and began to walk towards the edge of the party. She needed to think. They had precious few leads and only one more day before the River Killer's next set of victims.

"Sophie! Hold up there, cher."

Now several strides away from the other guests, Sophie bit her lip and folded her arms while her mother caught up.

Her mother huffed, chewing her own lip as she looked between Sophie and the commotion of the party beside them. She seemed to burst with the need to speak, but after several seconds, all she could manage were several false starts. "Sophie, I..." she tried once more.

"What? You what?" Sophie replied. Her shoulders bunched with the question. "Do you even know why I'm here? What happened in Peillon overnight?"

"Sophie, it's a party. We don't—"

"Word gets around fast. It got to me by seven in the morning, and I was all the way in Detroit, so you have to have heard."

Zadie winced, then replied softly, "Yes." She stepped closer, her voice dropping to nearly a whisper. "Those two girls. Found dead in the bayou."

"No," Sophie snapped. "Not *found dead*. Murdered. Two young women were murdered, Mama. Found on the river's edge with chains. Just like six years ago."

Blinking rapidly, Zadie brushed a fingertip along the edge of her eye. "Don't. Please, Sophie. Just—"

"Don't what?" Sophie interrupted. Her breath was starting to quicken, her jaw set. "Don't try to find their killer? Just let it go? Just like you and Daddy did with Molly?"

Zadie hugged herself, looking up at her daughter, her eyes begging her for something Sophie knew she couldn't give. "It's so ugly," her mother said at last. "Please, *mon petit,* we haven't seen you in years. Sit with me; have a cup of gumbo."

Sophie's neck tensed, she could feel her legs and arms coiling like a trap about to spring. "Do you know anyone who has been hanging around the Cotton House? Anyone out of the ordinary?"

Her head tilting in confusion, Zadie murmured, "What? The old hotel? No. What?"

"What about an old work van?" Sophie said, driving on, her voice cold and direct. "Anyone around here besides Victor that drives one? Or anywhere people have seen one they don't recognize?"

"Come inside. Have some coffee. If you still want to talk about your case, I—we—will. Listen, you hear that? Ti-Jean is gettin that guitar of his tuned up and then Carl'll break out that old accordion. You used to love singing along at these boils." Now Zadie's cheeks were flush as well. She stared into Sophie's eyes as if she were a kitchen cupboard, tossing the contents to find that one shaker of cayenne she knew she had but had somehow lost, buried behind the salt and flour.

But Sophie had gone frigid and still. "Chloroform. Their room reeked of it. Has anyone smelled it around? It's a weird thing to have. Has anyone in this town seen a man with a large bottle of chloroform or have you all been too busy peeling shrimp to notice?"

While Zadie had kept her voice low and hushed, Sophie now realized that the women gathered at her mother's lawn chairs were all staring at her. She had done nothing to lower her voice, and each eavesdropping ear had drawn its neighbor until Sophie realized a whole chorus of politely 'inattentive' ears filling the space between the buffet and the trailer door, all turned her direction.

Sophie met her mother's eye. Zadie lifted her chin, her eyes red and watery, but her lips now drew in a tight, defiant line. She was hurt. But the wound was already starting to scar... to numb itself. Recognition returning to remind her mother why they hadn't spoken in six years. Another disappointed face. Another immutable memory photographed and etched forever in Sophie's keen mind.

Turning on her heel, Sophie strode away. She took a long, looping path around the edge of the party, leaving the gossips and the quiet listeners behind. She walked with steady determined steps in a quick rhythm, using the sound of the gravel under her shoe to soothe herself.

True to her mom's word, a young man in a tank top with a colorful, loose-fitting button-up hanging open over it, Ti-Jean apparently, struck up a chord on his guitar and soon voices were singing a bright, jouncing tune while an accordion's merry huffing made its way in to support the melody.

Children with sparklers chased each other around with delighted squeals, barely watched by men and women engaged in their own mirthful conversations. Guffaws and clapped hands. The crunch of boiled corn on the cob and paper bags of cracklin passed around in tight circles of plastic chairs.

Even as Sophie reached the canal, she found that where a lower, earthy slope met the edge of the water, there were already children with rolled up pant-legs and skirts damp at the hem racing frogs and skipping stones across the wide face of the water.

That was what finally made Sophie stop.

She was staring down at a pair of little girls, they couldn't have even been in middle school yet. One had pigtails done up with a pair of pink ribbons to hide the hair ties that held them in place. The other's hair fell over her eyes over and over, prompting her to blow it out of her face with exaggerated huffs. They had found a sparkling stone in the canal. It looked like it might be quartz to Sophie, but the older of the two children adamantly told her pig-tailed companion that it was a magic crystal and they needed to find some herbs to make a witch's potion with it. It seemed a solid plan to Sophie, though the exact type of 'herb' had been left a mystery for the time being.

Twenty years ago, that could have been her and Molly. Down to the muddy dresses and magic potion. Sophie supposed the feeling she must be having was nostalgia, but as she went down the checklist of her own body language, her magician mentor, the Great Gavriel's, training painted a different story. Folded arms. Tight lips and narrow eyes. The sudden desire to avert her gaze.

Cold. Defensive.

Guilty.

Sophie gave the inside of her cheek a quick nip, using the shock to rouse herself. As she did, she heard footsteps in the grass behind her.

Greer stepped beside her, and Sophie stifled a laugh. Bermuda shorts hung as loose as swim trunks over his toned legs, and the fit FBI agent practically swam in a bright green t-shirt three sizes too large for him.

Scratching at his neck, he murmured. "I have some spare clothes back at the office. So I shouldn't need these very long."

"Are you sure?" Sophie teased. "I think it suits you. Sort of a 'tropical thug' look."

Greer smirked, giving back a short laugh.

"Yeah? My daughter is always saying I need to dress more hip if I want those dates."

"Not a fan of tan?" Sophie asked.

Greer shook his head. "Not as such. She's more a fan of dark leather jackets and silver chains."

"Sounds sweltering."

"She's seventeen. No discomfort is too great if it makes the look 'pop,'" Greer flared his fingers in front of him for emphasis.

"I remember being the age," Sophie consoled. "Eventually, you start valuing a pair of comfortable pants and supportive shoes over appreciative looks. Of course, I was in tights escaping water tanks and being sawn in half in front of a gawking audience at the time."

Greer blinked uncomprehendingly for a moment then shook his head. "Right. Sophie Quinn, celebrity magician. Hypnotist."

"Everyone starts somewhere."

A long pause stretched between them as the pair looked out over the children playing in the canal. A delighted roar and applause followed the back porch band as they swung the end of their last tune into the excited roil of the next. The smell of fish, garlic, onion, and a host of other frying delights was starting to draw Sophie's appetite more than she cared to admit. Her father wasn't wrong earlier. It was getting close to supper and she hadn't had more than coffee and her usual nutrition bar breakfast on the way to the Detroit field office that morning.

Coughing, Greer said, "Don't worry. I'll return the clothes to your folks myself. I know you're trying to get some space."

Sophie gripped her forearm, shrugging stiffly. She really didn't want to get into her parental issues with Greer. Despite his best intentions, there was simply no safe ground there.

"They seem nice," he added after another beat of silence.

Sophie gave a single, flat chuckle. "Yes. Nice is what they're about. Unfortunately, nice doesn't really deal well with reality. But if that's what you like, then yes, they are exceptionally nice."

Biting her lip, Sophie tilted her chin away from the blinding green of her partner's shirt. *Why did I say that? Just don't get into it, Soph. Just let it lie.*

Sophie took a deep breath and spoke again.

"I just don't get them. It's like they *want* to live like this."

"Like what?" Greer asked. She could tell from his tone what the older agent was hearing and seeing. He heard the music. The laughter. He saw the food and the party and the screaming children running roughshod over the grass. He didn't see the everyday threats and desperation creeping under the surface.

"Look at where you are," Sophie answered, her voice dropping. "This isn't a safe place. We've met one convicted felon next door and even he's scared someone more frightening is going to come in and break his legs. I grew up in Peillon. There's a hundred more Victor Hollands that you've walked by today and haven't even noticed. No doubt there's a couple dozen peeling crawfish at the party right now."

She gestured at the children and their parents at the edge of the canalway. "The only reason they aren't frightened every second of every day is because they're numb to it. They know there is evil here that they can't shut their doors against. That they can't protect themselves from. All they can do is smile. Throw crawdad boils. Play in the mud and don't worry about the gators."

Greer waited. Sophie stayed silent as well. She could tell that her accent was creeping out again, but she refused to acknowledge it. Refused to be embarrassed over her words. Staying had been a mistake, she should have just taken the towels and driven off as soon as the interview was over.

"You're talking about your sister," Greer said at last. Sophie clenched her jaw, but he continued. "She was living with them at the time, right? They couldn't protect her. You feel like it's their fault somehow?"

"I had been out for years," Sophie said. "I offered to buy them a mansion. God, back in those days, I was rolling in cash. *Mysteries and Phenomena* had just wrapped season one and I was doing a triple bill with the most famous illusionists in the world. I could have set them up anywhere, but they turned it down. No negotiation. No apology. Just 'No'."

Sophie began to pace now, walking up the canal edge, her back to her parent's trailer and the party, her voice raising to drown out the music from her own ears. "It's like living this way is a badge of honor for them. Like it makes them saints or martyrs or something. I don't know. I don't want to know. You know why? Because I gave them a chance for safety. A chance to be safe and free and comfortable, but instead, they stayed. They stayed until *he* came along and killed my sister. Living this way *killed* their daughter and they don't even have the guts to face it."

Suddenly they were at the car again. Sophie didn't realize she'd been walking that way, but as grass gave way to crunching gravel, she put her palms against the hood. She saw Greer reflected in the windshield. His face solemn, his expression stoic.

Great first impression, Soph.

Before either of them could speak again, Sophie's cell phone rang.

"Quinn, where the hell is Greer? I've been trying to reach him for ten minutes." Sophie abruptly spun to face the tall agent, and he hurriedly raised the green t-shirt, revealing his belt with his ID, pistol, and cell phone clip.

"He's here with me, ma'am," Sophie replied. Watching as Greer's cellphone came back to life in his hands. "He fell into the canalway pursuing a suspect and only just got his phone dried enough to power on again."

Merchant didn't bother keeping the surprise from her voice, "You have a suspect already?"

"Didn't pan out. But we have other—"

"Doesn't matter," the supervising agent interrupted. "Get to Gatlin Park. We have another body."

"Two more?" Sophie felt her heart plummet. Two women every two days, that was the River Killer's MO. To have them only a day apart...

"No," Merchant answered. "Just one."

Sophie's brow furrowed. "I don't understand."

"Neither do I. Now get down here and fast. If it's not connected, we have a much bigger problem on our hands."

Chapter 11

Between grasping branches hung a long, slender rope, like a fishing line descended from heaven, dropping from strong outstretched arms to dangle a young man upside down over the park trail.

Hickory, cypress, and ash filled out the parkland around the trail, reaching out for each other as if trying to shut out the dirt parking lot and narrow side roads leading back out to the main highway. Headlights from cop cars and two industrial standing lamps did their best to cover for the setting sun, who had clearly seen enough and was settling in for the final minutes of twilight. Sophie wished she could have done the same. But the scene in front of her told her she wouldn't be getting much sleep tonight anyway.

"What is going on?" Greer muttered, shutting the door of the white sedan behind him.

Sophie shook her head slowly. "This doesn't make any sense." Were there two killers loose in Peillon? She knew the River Killer's patterns.

She knew his techniques and the details of every victim from his first killings. And this... this wasn't right.

The pair circled the scene, paying mind to where the local PD had already set out little, numbered cones to mark potential evidence. As they approached, a thin man with a pencil mustache who looked the sort of twenty that still gets carded at bars swiftly approached. A brown, button-up uniform with a neat, black tie and a grey and gold patch marked him as part of the Sheriff's office, and before he even opened his mouth, Greer and Sophie held up their respective IDs.

"Agent Greer, FBI. This is Ms. Sophie Quinn, consulting. What do we have here?"

The young sheriff's deputy abruptly stopped, tipping his hat as if the fresh air might help him think how best to respond. He ran his eyes over Greer's baggy, green shirt and shorts and hooked his thumb into his belt, and for a moment, Sophie thought he might ask to see Greer's ID a bit closer.

Instead, he replied, "Deputy Cake," by way of introduction. "You must be the agents we were told were coming. Well, you better hurry. We're losing light by the minute and the ground's bare enough as it is."

Holding up a hand, Sophie looked back at the dirt parking lot and trodden ground around them. "Hold on. Before we go in, did you isolate any tracks in the area?"

"Tracks?" Deputy Cake replied, stroking his mustache. "What, you think a bear did this or something?"

"No," Sophie replied patiently. "Tire tracks. Tread. I doubt the killer marched our victim up the highway and down here on foot. Do we have any sign of the vehicle they took?"

Greer joined in, pulling up the pictures on his phone to refresh his memory. "We found evidence of a work van investigating the recent murders and if the same vehicle was here..." The agent left off the rest of the sentence, letting it hang meaningfully.

The deputy chewed at his cheek and shook his head. "I don't know anything about that. We were mainly worried about the body hanging over there. With the sun setting we had to scrounge up some lights."

Perfect. Sophie sighed. Greer similarly rubbed at his eyes, then waved a hand. "Nevermind. Just whoever's placing those markers, have them check around and mark any that don't match the police vehicles so I can compare them."

Continuing their walk to the hanging body, Deputy Cake gave a shrill whistle to another man in a Sheriff's uniform, this one wearing black gloves, and relayed the order.

"What do we know about the victim?" Greer asked.

Cake clicked his tongue. "Elijah Lambert. Twenty one. Lives in Peillon—"

"The Lambert place? Up on Sugar Hill Road?"

The deputy raised an eyebrow. "You know it?"

"I used to live here. I remember the Lamberts. Well to do. People respected them, that about right?"

"That's about the width of it," the deputy confirmed tilting his head. "Georgia Lambert has run of the place. Joseph senior shuffled off about eight years past and left it to her. We're informing his mother as we speak. Poor woman. Losing her daddy, then her husband, and now her son in less than ten years. Hard times but they do come." Deputy Cake turned and spat into the dirt beside him.

Sophie logged away that detail for later. Everything felt so off about this latest victim that her brain was working in overdrive trying to connect the dots.

Greer pointed up at the body. "Looks recent. Do we know how long he's been here?"

The victim hung upside down with his arms freely dangling. His fingertips were five feet off the ground with the rope looping on a branch ten feet above him. His stomach was exposed, showing pale, bloodless skin in the light of the industrial lamps above the bunching of his shirt as it rolled towards his armpits. The shirt itself was stained with red.

"Apparent cause of death seems to be blood loss from a slice across the jugular vein," commented the deputy. "Now hold up here." Putting out a hand, Cake gestured to the ground. "We got some blood splatter we noticed, but we're still trying to figure it out." All around the hanging body, small orange cones marked dark streaks in the dirt and dead foliage.

"That has to be a twenty-foot radius," Greer noted.

Nodding along, Cake added, "We figure they must have scrapped for a bit after the victim took that slash to his throat. I don't know how else you get that much blood all over the ground."

Sophie squinted at the series of stains then up at the body again.

"Deputy Cake, may I borrow your flashlight?"

With a click and a twist, the thin man handed over a heavy, mallet-shaped piece and the trio followed the beam as Sophie shined the light on the tree branches above.

"Look at that wear," she said. "See in the bark?"

Greer nodded. The deputy squinted further.

"It's like the rope was scraping the branch all around it. And look." She dropped the beam to the victim's body. "No blood on his chest, just on his throat and the ground."

Greer's eyes shot wide. "Wait." Holding up a palm, he turned and rushed back for the car. The deputy looked between Sophie and her retreating partner, the confusion apparent on his face.

"I take it y'all have a theory?"

Sophie traced the spread of orange cones marking major blood splatter on the ground with the flashlight's beam. As she did, she explained, "He wasn't slashed and then hung. He was strung up and then slashed. If he had been cut beforehand blood would be all over his chest and pants, but it's only on his shirt, around his throat, and across the ground. The blood is spread wide because as he was bleeding to death, the killer pushed the rope. He sent Elijah spinning in a long circle, a spiral."

"Jesus... Why would he do a thing like that?"

Looping the flashlight through the spiral, Sophie swallowed hard. Why, indeed? RK used chains. He used games. There wasn't anything clever about stringing a man up and slitting his throat. And the spiral only had an aesthetic twinge to its execution, like an artistic choice or perhaps a compulsion.

Greer came back, his laptop open in his hands and throwing digital light up under his jaw in an image like a jack o'lantern's smile.

"Hoffrey Timms," he said hurriedly, his face grim.

The name immediately sparked in Sophie's mind. That was what had bothered her about the crime scene.

She'd seen it before.

"No," said Sophie. "That's impossible."

"What? What's impossible? Who's Geoffrey Tim?" Deputy Cake interjected, his hands on his hips as he craned his neck to get a look at Greer's screen.

"Hoffrey Timms," Greer said, "The Butcher of Memphis. He's a serial killer, convicted for a string of murders in and around Tennessee. He lured young men into secluded areas, parks and the like, then he would hang them and cut their throats. Leave them to bleed like hogs."

Sophie gestured from the victim to the blood. "He would set the victims spinning as they bled to make these spiral patterns under them. I've heard that it helps the blood to drain more quickly, but interviews with Timms always made it seem like he just liked the design."

Deputy Cake ran a finger between his neck and collar, stretching the neck of his uniform. "And you think this is our guy?"

"No," Sophie said quickly. "It doesn't add up."

"Why not?"

"Because," Greer tapped the laptop screen, letting the pair look more closely. "Hoffrey Timms has been on death row for the last fifteen years. Records show he's still there too."

Letting out a long, low whistle, Deputy Cake removed his hat and gave his head a quick scratch. "That throws a wrench in things. So where does that leave us?"

Greer's eyes narrowed as he closed his laptop, slinging it up under one arm. "Two killers showing up at the same time, both of them sharing the methods of well-known serial killers from the past. The odds of that being true are small. Not impossible. But small. If I had to say right now, I'd wager we have a copycat on our hands."

Sophie closed her eyes. Her stomach knotted itself and she felt her mouth pinching into a grimace. That couldn't be true. It had all fit. The first two victims had matched RK's MO. He was back. He had to be back. How could she catch him if it wasn't even *him*?

Red light from a cigar flashed behind Sophie's eyes. A voice in her mind.

His voice. Graveled. Dragged in a soft Cajun near enough to her own.

Eh. That's just too bad, isn't it, cher? You're free. That was the deal, no? A better deal than those other girls got, no doubt-about it. You and me, huh? Both free.

Sophie bit down on the inside of her cheek. She tasted blood. Felt the sharp pain drag her up and out of the voice's taunting like a fish on a hook.

"No," Sophie said, her voice hard. She folded her arms, looking up at Greer. "No."

The tall agent's jaw slid side to side as he met her gaze. But Sophie did not turn away.

Another deputy called out and Sophie heard a muttered apology as Deputy Cake tipped his hat and jogged to the edge of the floodlights.

Sophie paid no mind to the man's retreat. Her eyes linked with the crystal blue of Greer's.

"What are you thinking, Miss Quinn?" the fit agent said, his voice dropping.

"It has to be him," Sophie said, her words quick and clipped.

Greer shook his head, "It doesn't add up. This second killing is too different. It's a completely separate killer's methods."

"He's messing with us," Sophie replied, exasperation climbing into her throat. "He's been planning his comeback for six years. He thinks he's some sort of clever genius, and he wants to trick us. He wants to run us back and forth, but I know it's him."

"Quinn, see reason here," Greer leaned back on his heels, replying in a stage whisper. "What do we know? Serial killers have egos. They evolve at the start, but once they embrace their methods and their identity, they stick to them religiously. They can't handle having someone else take the credit. So what makes more sense, that someone so self-absorbed and egotistical would abandon their previous methods and start over after six years, all for the *sole* purpose of tricking *you* specifically, or that we have a copycat killer taking notes from famous serial killers?"

Sophie was shaking, her hands fell to her sides as she picked at the inside of her fingernails. She didn't know what to say. It made sense. If she were in Greer's shoes, she would probably be making the same arguments. But it couldn't be true. It felt so wrong. So hollow.

Finally, she said, "You don't know him like I do."

With an explosive sigh, Greer replied, "Well, maybe that's a good thing in this case. I think he's poisoned your thinking here. We have to look where the evidence points, and right now, it's not pointing to RK."

A tense silence stretched between them, punctuated by the snap and flash of the forensics team taking pictures.

"Agent Greer!" Deputy Cake waved from the mouth of the trail. "We've found some tire treads if you want to get a look."

Greer held up a finger, lingering a moment as he looked anywhere but back into the hard line of Sophie's stare.

"Listen," he said softly. "I'm going to look around here a bit more, but it's getting late. We'll regroup tomorrow. Here, take the car. Get some supper. I'll get one of the local boys to drop me off and set up a couple rooms at the motel for the night. The Creek Bed Motel. You know where it is?"

Sophie nodded and Greer returned the gesture. He looked as if he might say something else, but instead, he turned and headed off to join the deputies by their alleged tire tracks.

Finding a bite to eat would be easy. Sophie still knew the layout around Main Street and what diners had been around when she had been a teenager here. But she'd keep it short. There was another errand pulling her attention.

Pulling away, the sedan headlights caught the slope of the rising road in front of her and the distant tree tops of Sugar Hill.

She'd give the Lamberts another half hour for their own dinner. Then, Sophie had some questions for the family of Elijah Lambert...

The River Killer's latest victim.

Chapter 12

After years of disappointment, Sophie compartmentalized the private eyes she worked with by two criteria. First, did they take more time to ask questions about the case or to negotiate their fees and stipends. Second, how quickly do they answer their phones in the odd hours of the day.

Fabian St. Claire's fee had a tendency to fluctuate, but he discussed it with the brevity of a waiter dropping off the check at the end of a meal. And while he never answered his phone, the man's return calls invariably came back in under three minutes.

Sitting in Greer's white sedan on the edge of the historic property the Lambert family had held since its foundations were laid down over a hundred years ago, Sophie waited for her cell phone to ring.

Two minutes, ten seconds. A single chime, and Sophie lifted the phone to her cheek.

"Miss Sophie, a pleasure to hear from you again. It has been too long, no?" The silk-smooth voice on the line affected the indulgent tones of a long-expected friend with a Southern drawl that teased a line between Texas grit and the more Arcadian notes of the Gulf end of the Mississippi Basin.

"Fabian," Sophie acknowledged. "You received my message?"

The voice on the line chuckled. "It's coming, Miss Sophie. I admit, I was surprised. Last I heard you were gone to greener pastures. But, suppose I'm the fool for expecting that to keep you away. Ah well, such is *la destinée*."

Sophie grimaced. She knew the PI and bounty hunting circles cooperated and shared information when it suited them, so it shouldn't come as a shock that her previous informants would know she'd spent the last year and a half in Detroit by now.

Adjusting her grip on the phone, Sophie answered, "New developments pulled me back. But we're not here to talk about that right now. I'm only interested in the Lambert family. Elijah in particular. Do you have a dossier on them?"

A momentary pause, a click like the sound of someone rattling a cough drop behind their teeth. Then Fabian St. Claire sighed. "I do," he said. "And you have my fee?"

Sophie turned her phone again, the bright light of a banking interface swept up, following her fingers. She tried not to pay attention to the numbers in the available balance. She never had before. When she was starting out, getting her degree in criminology, doing her own initial investigations, her tv money had still been rolling in. Then she coasted on a few of her last stage show payouts and the sale value of her California mansion. She could afford to hire teams of private investigators to follow the barest whiff of a trail in those days. Now... well, the coiling in her stomach cautioned discretion.

As the payment confirmed, an email popped into Sophie's phone inbox, and Fabian picked up the conversation.

"Nothing too unusual. You know the family is old money around here. Georgia Lambert lost her husband and got the manor house after her pops, Joseph Senior, died."

Sophie looked out the window at the broad-faced, two-story house. The sweeping front porch met red-brick walkways, and the oval wall of a glittering sunroom reached from one front corner to the back like a decorative sash on a dignitary. The paint was chipped at the edges and the interior lights showed where smudges lingered in the glass.

Loss of fortune showed itself around the trimmed lawn. Sophie could see the bare, ruddy ground where gardens had been pulled up rather than being left to seed and knew that what she'd heard from the deputy was right. Hard times had come to the house of Lambert.

"And Elijah?" Sophie prompted, pulling up the file on her phone as she listened to her PI.

"The usual sort of roughhousing and trouble you'd expect," Fabian explained. "Lost his father five years ago. His family shares the home with his aunt and uncle, a few cousins, and, of course, his sister, Marie."

Sophie nodded, lingering on the picture of a girl with shoulder-length, brown hair and a haughty smile. It seemed to be taken from a high-school yearbook.

"Sophie?"

"Hmm?" she paused. Fabian's playful voice had gone serious for a moment.

"Be careful, yes?"

"Fabian, I'm always careful." Was that concern in his voice?

A digitized sigh. "Of course. But... three deaths in two days?"

"Goodnight, Fabian."

Sophie ended the call. With a final look at the file, she took a steadying breath and got out of the car.

***

A grim-faced man in his forties answered the door. His expression as weary as the whining hinges of the screen door he propped open. His shoulders hunched, half by the exhaustion apparent in his stance and partly by his lanky height that forced him to slouch under the door's head.

Uncle Eugene, Sophie thought, the picture leaping from Fabian's dossier in her memory.

"Apologies for interrupting your evening," Sophie began. "I'm Sophie Quinn with the FBI, I'm here to ask—"

"I know what you're here for," the man barked. "You're late. Already spoke to the police. Talked with them the last few hours. My sister is inconsolable, finally lying down for a rest, but here you are. Do you have any leads? Any additional information at all or are you just here to ask the same stupid questions all over so that you can tell your boss you did something?"

Sophie nodded sympathetically. Talking to friends and family still fresh with the trauma of death was never ideal, but time was short. There were answers she needed. "I can't imagine how hard this must be for her, for all of you," she replied gently.

"No. You can't," the man confirmed. His shirt was unbuttoned at the throat and wrinkled around the cuffs and waist, and he leaned forward like the shadow of a gargoyle threatening the pedestrians crossing under his disgusted gaze.

The man was trying to assert control. It was a common coping mechanism and one Sophie had seen many times before. When everything was out of control, some people leaned hard into their pessimism, as if predicting failure and abandoning hope could shield them from the pain and cruelty of life.

Sophie let the man's words hang, her eyes lowering and her hands folding as if consenting to the man's despair. Really she used the moment to discretely look past him. In the wide, hardwood foyer behind him, Sophie caught shadows of movement. Other people in an adjacent living room leaning to listen but keeping quiet to not draw attention to themselves.

They were gathered together. That was a good sign. People gathered for comfort, but also to share their suspicions, their worries and fears. They may be primed to speak, if Sophie could reach them.

"I only have a few questions. I'm part of the special team assigned to your nephew's murder, and I'd like to sit with you all."

Technically, she and Greer were assigned to follow up the RK murders, but Sophie suspected this family may be more cooperative if they believed they were receiving special and 'complete' attention.

Sophie inclined her shoulder, a subtle motion, a silent cue that she was walking in. Most people reflexively move out of the way, and Uncle Eugene was no different. Shifting back on his heel, Sophie walked past the man, registering the glower on his lips as he stomped around her towards the group gathered in the living room.

A gaggle of young Lamberts between the ages of ten and nineteen hung over high-backed chairs and embroidered couches designed for elegance and opulence rather than comfort. Mostly Aunt Flora's children. But between a cold fireplace and a window-mounted AC unit struggling against the summer heat sat a young woman in an open-back top and jean shorts that Sophie recognized from the dossier as Marie, Elijah's sister, and now Georgia Lambert's sole living child.

Her curtain of lively, brown hair hung over her face and obscured the glimmering trails of tears running between her eyes and jawline.

Catching Sophie's gaze, Marie quickly wiped at her cheek and looked away into the stone hollow of the dark fireplace.

"This is Agent Quinn," Eugene announced, folding his arms. "She has a few more questions."

"Well, that's fantastic, I'm sure we all have some questions for her too."

Sophie registered the voice was from a heavy-set woman with a high set bun and an open container of mixed nuts set on the end table beside her overstuffed chair. Aunt Flora, Uncle Eugene's wife. The woman gave a polite smile, but her eyes narrowed as she glanced between Eugene and Sophie. Eugene returned the look with a shrug.

Cracking open a pistachio, Aunt Flora gestured to the couch. "Edgar, Morris, get up, let the lady policeman have a seat. Now tell me, what have you found out?"

Without waiting for an answer, Eugene and the younger Lambert cousins all leapt into the verbal fray, assaulting Sophie with a wall of sound and angry inquiry.

"Do you know who did it?" "Any witnesses yet?" "It was Gatlin Park, people jog there all the time! How can no one have seen anything?" "What are you doing here? Didn't anyone tell you we already talked to the police?"

Holding up a hand, Sophie tried to slow down the pace of the questions, but the Lambert clan seemed far more interested in venting their anxiety on her than actually receiving answers to their volleyed questions.

"We're investigating all possible angles," Sophie interjected. Then, more forcefully, she added, "I'm part of a newly created task force to—"

"You said that already," Eugene roared, his heavy voice rising over the cacophony of his own children and wife. "What does that even mean? Are the regular police not looking anymore? Are you the only one trying to find my nephew's killer?"

"Who even are you?" Flora asked with a dismissive sneer and a twist of her wrist.

This was getting out of control. Straightening her back, Sophie spread her arms, instantly creating space around herself, lifting her chin as she drew up a breath from deep inside her chest. "Alright. That's enough."

Her voice was clear and resonant as a bell, sharp and precise with a command that could hold the attention of thousands from a theater stage. Sophie had worked for years without the benefit of microphones, and the Great Gavriel had taught her how to push her voice, speaking from the diaphragm and asserting herself. She wasn't just speaking to be heard but to bring every murmuring heckler and bored teen out of their iPhone and into the show, *her* show.

"I'm Sophie Quinn. I'm the investigator assigned to Elijah's case. And the sooner I ask these questions, the sooner we *will* find his killer. I promise you that."

The room fell quiet, and Sophie looked from eye to eye. She lingered a moment as she found Marie's gaze once more. The young girl's eyes were red. Her lip quivered, and she quickly ducked her chin, averting her stare once more as she wrapped her arms around her knees and pulled herself behind the screen of her long, dark hair.

The silent actions spoke volumes to Sophie. Concealing motions. Withdrawing. Either the girl was a card-carrying introvert of the highest degree, or she knew something. Something she wanted to keep from the police and, thereby, Sophie. Perhaps something she wanted to keep from her family?

Marie would be the key, Sophie felt with growing confidence. But how would she get to her through her family?

A voice from the hallway drew the group's attention.

"Sophie Quinn?"

A woman in a silk nightgown that covered her from wrists to ankles, her hair frazzled, her eyes bloodshot with spent tears, stepped from an adjoining stairwell into the living room. Her voice was coarse and Sophie could hear the ragged aftermath of screams and sobbing in her words.

Georgia Lambert. Elijah's mother.

"It is you," Georgia whispered. "I've seen you before. Your show, *Mysteries and Phenomena with Sophie Quinn*. I watched every episode. I've even seen your stage show before."

The teenage Lamberts exchanged murmured words and pulled out cellphones as they each corroborated their aunt's comment in their own way.

Sophie's heart stopped. Meeting a fan was always treacherous ground. Her show was designed to capitalize on her skills as a hypnotist and a magician, to play up the 'dark mysteries' that hung between clever stage magic and the unexplainable. Aliens. Psychics. ESP. It was really unsurprising that despite Sophie's implications that her talents were purely human, many of her fans insisted that she possessed powerful psychic abilities.

Sometimes even telling a fan to their face that she couldn't speak with the dead or read their minds would only elicit a pitying wink and an implication that her producers, or perhaps the government or even the Illuminati, were preventing her from telling the truth.

It was dangerous ground, and looking at the sudden wonder on Georgia Lambert's face, Sophie had a feeling which type of fan she was.

Sophie stepped to meet the grieving woman. "It's a pleasure to meet you, Mrs. Georgia, and I wish we had met under happier circumstances." Taking her hands, Sophie gave her a reassuring squeeze. "I'm so sorry that this happened to you. But I'm with the FBI and I'm here to help."

Georgia looked as if she may burst into tears afresh, but she returned the squeeze and shook her head enthusiastically.

"Yes. Yes, of course. Anything you need."

"You can't be serious," said Eugene, a bitter mutter in his voice.

Georgia shot him a glare. "Eugene, if you don't have anything constructive to add, I'm sure there are other places you can be."

Her brother rolled his eyes. "Georgia, this is real-life. A psychic? Really?"

Georgia turned her back on her brother, focusing on Sophie again. "I know you can help. I know you don't like doing them, and I wouldn't ask if it wasn't so important, but it's my son. Please!"

Her stomach dropped, and Sophie felt her fingertips go cold. She could sense how Georgia thought she could help, and she had a feeling it didn't lie in precise questioning and diligent forensics. "Mrs. Lambert, I am here to help, but I'm with the FBI and—"

"Yes! I know, and I won't tell them, I swear. I can even pay you if you like."

"Georgia!" Eugene shouted.

"This is my son, Eugene!"

A furious silence stretched in the air as the grieving mother let out a hiccupping sob. Her hands were trembling. Sophie lowered her voice, speaking at an intimate, conversational volume. It seemed she wouldn't have a choice, but maybe there was a way through here. A way to get what she needed too.

"You want a reading," she said, softly. "You want me to do a séance for your son."

Georgia tried to speak, once, twice, then lowered her head and nodded.

"We told the police everything," Georgia murmured. "And it wasn't enough. Only one person can help us now. Elijah. Only Elijah knows what happened to him. Please, Ms. Quinn, you have to help us. Help my son."

Sophie let go of Georgia's hands. She stepped around her to the edge of the room. The horror and trauma was fresh in Georgia's mind. She was still riding the jagged edge of an experience her body hadn't quite accepted wasn't a nightmare.

This was dangerous. Leveraging people's belief in the supernatural was irresponsible. Sophie had only done a couple of spook shows on *Mysteries and Phenomena*. They always did well, and the producers suggested them every season, but they left her feeling... oily... soiled, by the end.

But what other options did she have?

"All right," Sophie said at last. "On two conditions."

Georgia nodded her head rapidly, her frazzled hair bouncing over her eyes with the frantic motion. "Yes, anything."

"First, we'll need a quiet space. Peace and calm are key, at least, as much as can be managed."

"Of course," Georgia took Sophie by the elbow, leading her towards the hallway again. "We can use the dining room. It's the far side of the house, so no one will disturb us," she said, glancing meaningfully at her brother and the rest of the assembled Lamberts.

"That will be fine," Sophie replied, gingerly slowing down Georgia's exit. "Second, the circle will be strongest if those closest to him are there. Marie?"

The other Lambert sibling looked up from the empty fireplace, her cheeks flushing red at the sudden attention. Sophie tilted her head with a reassuring smile. "Will you join us?"

Chapter 13

Georgia Lambert's fingers clenched and unclenched in anxious expectation. Her daughter Marie's touch was light, still, like a rabbit at the sound of distant wings. Together with Sophie, the three women sat alone at a table made for a family. Hands linked, cold despite the lingering heat of the day.

Sophie knew the touch, the look in the young woman's downcast eyes. Marie was already seeing ghosts in her own mind, and they had nothing to do with the lone sandalwood candle the family had scrounged up for the task or the fingertip drizzling of nighttime rain tapping the wood siding and high-topped windows of the historic, Southern house.

In the dark, together, hands held and space left for the spirits who would join them, Sophie took a deep, performative breath that reinforced the silence behind the candle's gently crinkling flame.

"I feel him," Sophie said, balancing the elements of invitation and command in her voice.

Sophie felt the tremor in Georgia Lambert's hand that she had been expecting. And in her other hand, Marie stiffened.

She hated it, the deception of it all. If she could have gotten Marie away from her family, perhaps she could have eased her mind enough for the girl to open up. But there was no time. No time to break her mother of her misconceptions about Sophie's abilities. No time to convince the family that her help didn't come from a supernatural place. No time if she wanted to save another life.

Just one more smear on her karma that she would have to bear.

A choked gasp came from Georgia. "E...Elijah? Is that really you?"

Sophie lowered her chin, taking another breath, this time to stifle the glimmering of a tear in her own eye, her heart breaking for the woman beside her. She had to hold it together. Marie knew something and more lives may depend on it.

"I see him. Thin, athletic..." Sophie had seen as much at the crime scene but establishing trust was important. They needed to believe her words were coming from him. The moment they suspected a trick, it would all be over.

"That's Elijah," Georgia confirmed, a sniffle and a shake of her head. "Is he saying anything? What... what's he doing?"

Sophie gave her hand another reassuring shake. "He's trying to show me something. He's showing me... a book, like a journal? No... thicker, a box... a box with money in it?"

Sophie had taken a guess. Secrets people kept in their own minds were generally safe. But if someone else knew... like a sister... chances were the secret had some physical element to it. And when someone was hiding something, there were two main places for a mentalist to look, written in their diaries and journals or hidden away in some safe storage box. Marie had not reacted to the mention of a journal, but the tremble in her arms at the mention of a box was unmistakable.

From there, money was the likely guess. It had been a hard few years for the Lambert family. The disrepair of the property, the passing of two of the family's providers in the span of eight years. It wasn't unreasonable to imagine a young man doing something secretive to help his family... or himself.

"Money?" Georgia whispered. "I don't understand. What does a box of money have to do with... Elijah?"

Marie shook the long hair from her face, looking into the candle with a new-found intensity. She blinked rapidly, and Sophie could see her lips hesitating on the edge of speech as Elijah's sister struggled to hold back tears of her own.

Sophie looked into the candle as well, directing nothing towards Marie, giving no sign that she saw the girl's silent struggle. She was on the edge...

All she needed was a small push.

"He lied about where he was going," Sophie tested. "He was meeting someone. Someone new... an opportunity."

Marie let out a choked scream as the candle flickered in front of them. Her chair fell back, and the young woman snatched her hands away.

Georgia gasped, and the last ounce of Marie's resolve evaporated. Her face crumbled like a toddler's, dissolving into tears.

"He said it would be safe!" she gasped, her voice now croaking with barely contained sobs.

Georgia's eyes went wide with horror. "Marie?"

"He said they did this all the time," Marie said. Wrapping her arms around herself, she looked from Sophie to her mother and back. "He just wanted to help. He knew we were almost out of money. After Daddy's death, we got some from the insurance, but with Mama's health... and Uncle Eugene still trying to get his business going... it's hard for all of us. He just wanted to help..."

Rounding the table, Georgia put her arms around her daughter. "It's ok, honey. It's ok. I'm here."

Sophie stayed seated. "Why did Elijah go out today?" she asked, calmly.

Marie shook her head, pulling back from her mother. Shame. Fear.

Guilt.

Sophie remembered when she was Marie's age, a little younger than her actually... barely fifteen but pouring every hour she could into practicing with Gavriel. She hadn't done it for money, not directly anyway. She swept the stage and cleaned the props for training. For the skills that would let her escape. Once she could perform her own shows, she could escape the trailer… escape Peillon. It sounded like Elijah was trying to do the same, perhaps hoping to take his mother and sister with him, but trying to escape the grip of impending poverty all the same.

"Who was he meeting?" Sophie prompted.

Marie swallowed, taking a breath as she steadied herself against her mother. "Cash Calloway," she said at last. "He runs riverboat tours. We don't get a lot of tourists around here… not usually. But Elijah said he poaches gators sometimes. I know it's illegal, but it's good money and you hear about it sometimes. It didn't seem… He was supposed to meet up today. Show him the ropes. I—" Marie swallowed, her eyes squinting together as her words collapsed in tears that wouldn't be held back any longer. "I don't think he knew Elijah told me. It was a secret."

As Sophie left the mother and daughter together in the sandalwood-scented dark, she wondered briefly if she ought to turn the lights on as she left.

Ultimately, she was glad she had kept the candlelit darkness. Settling into Greer's sedan and plugging Cash Calloway's name into the FBI databases, her thoughts were better suited to the blackness of night.

Chapter 14

Stealing watercraft was becoming something of a habit for Sophie. But as she glanced at the phone in her hand and saw the hour swiftly approaching midnight, she decided this was yet another 'ask forgiveness instead of permission' situation.

The outboard motor on the small jonboat chuffed along enthusiastically, and the croak of crickets and bullfrogs in the tall grass surrounding the riverway had a soothing effect that counteracted the sour scent stirred up from the algae breaking under the boat's flat prow.

Cash Calloway's river tour dock was predictably closed, and the attached cabin, which Sophie's research confirmed acted as Calloway's primary residence, had met her knocking with silent indifference. It didn't take much imagination to guess where Calloway might be, with his cabin sitting empty and dark and loose cabling hanging where a boat should be docked.

The *complete* picture was fuzzy in Sophie's mind. The poacher might not have anything to do with Elijah Lambert's death. But it was more than passing strange to think that the day Elijah was set to start his new—secret—job was the same day he was randomly chosen by an obsessive, methodical killer. No, there would be some connection here. Sophie just needed to discover what it was.

Sophie glanced down at her phone again.

Greer had texted her the motel room numbers an hour ago. In the moment, Sophie had wondered what the handsome agent might say if she told him where she was. Would he come along to help? Remembering the way Greer had picked the lock on Victor Holland's trailer door, a part of her suspected he would. The other part of her remembered the reluctance and distrust on the drive to the Cotton House, not to mention the bitter words exchanged at the scene of Elijah Lambert's death.

She had sent a quick thanks, offering no explanation for where she was, and after watching 'Greer is typing' flit on and off of her screen for the better part of a minute, Sophie had simply pocketed her phone and tried not to give the man another thought.

After all, it wasn't like she was helpless on her own. She was fit and had received some FBI training. It wasn't that many years ago that she'd been kickboxing and running every day to practice for the entrance exams. She needed to stay in shape for the stage and this had just been a further extension in that direction. If anything, trying to coordinate with a partner that she didn't know and didn't fully trust could compromise her focus. What if they got in each other's way and someone got hurt... or worse, they lost the suspect?

No, it was better to take this on her own.

Besides, apart from perhaps a gun, the only thing she might need would be a pair of cuffs, and Greer had left a spare set in the console of his sedan.

On the better-patrolled stretches of the canals, Sophie cut her engine. Paddling or drifting on the current to avoid the odd junction too close to a road or a known patrol boat trap, she made her way in a winding search grid. She'd likely hear Calloway before she saw him anyway. No quiet way to hunt gator.

Alligator poaching had been a problem as long as Sophie could remember. The leather, the teeth, and the meat all commanded a price, and to protect the ecosystem and stop them from being hunted to extinction, strict hunting seasons were enforced. Add to this the fact that hunting licenses were so in demand that they were actually assigned by lottery and it was no wonder that a persistent black market survived all along the Mississippi delta.

Long minutes crept by on the sporadic flares of fireflies, each second ticking with the gentle tap of drizzling rain. The overreaching tree limbs blocked the meager rain, leaving a misting haze over the sluggish bayou water.

A flashlight flared between the trees, and Sophie dropped low.

"Sonnuvabitch!" called a voice around the nearest bend in the lazy river. "C'mere!"

Her engine silent, Sophie paddled closer, following the sweeping light as it rolled up and down. She caught the silhouette of a man standing beside the fan of a silent airboat, perhaps fifty meters away. He swayed from the buoying water under the metal floor, and she heard the rough *plunk* of his boots hitting the flat steel.

She couldn't see his face in the dark, but the flailing light showed brief glimpses of a red t-shirt and worn jeans. Then Sophie saw why the man was fumbling so much with his flashlight.

A shotgun perched in the crook of his elbow.

A calamitous blast shook Sophie and sent her hands rushing to her ears. She fell to the floor of the jonboat as a splash of water flew up in a geyser in front of the man.

Her breath came in quick, sharp gasps. Sophie's vision swam as tunnel vision narrowed her view to the sliver of moon peeking between the drizzling clouds and fragmented treetops.

Fly free, little angel, the voice in her head taunted.

And Sophie felt herself falling, falling into icy cold. Her clothing was heavy, suffocating her. She kicked her leg, feeling the clink of a chain at her ankle.

It's not real, she thought. *I'm not there.* But it felt real. The bayou shifted around her. The little jonboat expanded until it could fit the terrified figure of Molly sitting in a hallucinatory chair. Summer lightning bugs became the red smolder of an evil cigar between malicious lips.

No!

Sophie's heart raced. Her hands shook.

... and then she tasted blood.

With a gasp, Sophie shoved herself to her knees. She was in the jonboat again. Alone. She dabbed her lips with the back of her hand and caught a glimmering streak of red that she quickly wiped away on her pant leg.

The sting on the inside of her cheek was a lingering reminder of the trick that could save her from these flashbacks.

Grabbing the outboard motor like a lifeline, Sophie closed her eyes.

The shotgun let out another blast.

She knew now that the shooter wasn't aiming at her. He was distracted.

Poaching gators.

Tearing at the ignition, Sophie adjusted the little boat's course. There was no more need for subtlety. No desire for it either. She felt raw, her nerves ragged.

She picked up speed, a shark-fin wake tearing up behind her as she leaned into the boat's turn around the bend in the bayou, keeping it upright as it threatened to roll.

The flashlight shook and then turned up in her direction.

"What the hell!" shouted a gruff voice.

The light was blinding, but Sophie didn't need to see. Instead, she took the final image in her mind's eye, the open water between her and the airboat. Factoring in the speed of her current course, her sense of timing honed by countless hours of practice, Sophie waited until the boats were on top of each other, no slowing down, no change in direction... and she jumped.

Metal bit metal with a screaming *gronk!* as the boats collided at ramming speeds. The momentum throwing itself behind Sophie's jump, she hurdled into the poacher's airboat. One forearm up to shield her face, the other arm drawn back like a coiled spring, she smashed into the man like a pouncing tiger, both of them tumbling to the floor of the airboat as the rear of her johnboat rose out of the water and spun to collide with the rear fan's cage. Water flew up around them and the small engine sputtered before dropping back to a murmuring idle.

"Get offa me!" the coarse voice shouted from under her. The flashlight fell and rolled to the side, illuminating the inner wall of the airboat, and Sophie's eyes went night-blind from the sudden shift of light to darkness. Still running on instinct, Sophie sent the heel of her hand forward in a sharp strike, finding cheekbone. She didn't wait to see the impact of her initial blow, raising a hand for a second strike.

Suddenly the metal barrel of the shotgun slammed up into her stomach with the sudden force of a seatbelt in a car crash. Sophie gasped, her stomach tensing at the pain. The man under her was trying to shove her off, holding the shotgun up between them like a barricade.

Blinking rapidly to try and acclimate her eyes, Sophie found the poacher's wrists by touch. She jammed her thumbs into the tendons, and the man let out an animal scream as the firearm suddenly shuddered and fell out of fingers as loose as noodles.

Sophie tossed the shotgun overboard with one hand while the other fished out the cuffs from her pocket.

She had to end this—fast.

The man was no longer fighting back, only trying to scramble out from under her. A knee shot up, throwing her off balance, and she fought to stay perched over the man's chest.

There was no way she'd get both his wrists together, as wildly as he was fighting. Surprise had been spent, soon he'd rally and this would turn into a more even fight than Sophie wanted.

Instead, moving on instinct, Sophie pulled back. She let the man scramble backward, pushing with his palms and heels as he moved away from her. As he did, she didn't reach for his hands, instead, Sophie hooked the cuff around an ankle, popping the other link of the cuff around the steel leg of one of the airboat's passenger chairs.

He jerked, once, twice, grunting as the cuff bit into his heel. Sophie stood with a long, steadying sigh, scooping up the flashlight as she did.

Pinning the light onto the man's face, she looked beyond the scruff of untrimmed beard and the furious pinch of the eyebrows, matching the eyes, the nose, the overall shape and dimensions of the face with the driver's license photo in the FBI database.

"Cash Calloway," she said at last. "I'm here to talk about Elijah Lambert."

Chapter 15

"If you are very lucky, this night is going to end with you in a jail cell." Sophie sat back in one of the airboat's passenger chairs. Her voice was clear and unapologetic as she looked around the metal hull with feigned disinterest.

There were no other guns that she could see. His shotgun sunk to the bottom of the bayou, Cash Calloway's t-shirt and jeans didn't leave room to conceal much more than a pocketknife, but the way she'd cuffed his ankle to the airboat didn't set that possibility as much of a threat.

A cooler of cheap beer, a pole with a metal hook for wrangling dead gators into the boat, and a stinking bait bucket with fist-sized hunks of chicken and beef were all safely behind Sophie's seat and well out of her suspect's reach.

So far, Cash had limited his responses to glares, but after this last comment, he spat at her.

"Bullshit," he snarled. "Crazy bitch. You attacked me. I don't know what you think you saw, but this is police brutality."

Sophie leaned back. Acutely aware of the moonlight over her, she angled her chin to put her face in shadow. The darkness, and a slight widening of the eyes, made the glint in her irises pop and gave her the cat-eyed look of a predator.

It was a look she'd perfected for close-up shots and Halloween specials.

"I'm not a cop," she said, her voice, intimate, sotto voce against the rippling water. "It's true, I do work with them. But no one knows I'm here. No one even knows to look for you. That's kind of the idea of your job, isn't it? Poaching? So if I were in your position," she gestured to the cuff around his ankle, "I would stop worrying about what's legal, and start wondering how I can convince this crazy woman I'm worth the trouble of arresting."

Cash swallowed hard, looking around at the dark silhouettes of the cypress trees, moss hanging like the cobwebs of enormous spiders. Sophie could see in his face, the way he glanced at the gator hooks behind her, he was still thinking about escape. If he got the chance, he'd attack her again. She needed him to focus.

"Elijah Lambert," she said flatly.

"I told you, I've never heard of the guy," Cash insisted, adjusting his leg with a groan and sending a chime through the cuff's ring.

Sophie shook her head. "You were supposed to meet with him today. He thought he was going to poach alligator with you."

Scratching at his scruffy beard, Calloway's eyes narrowed. "Says who? They're lying."

"Don't play games with me, Cash. We both know Elijah Lambert left his home this afternoon to meet you, and then a few hours later, he's found dead. So tell me. What happened when you saw him?"

Cash's mouth flapped like a fish, but only for a moment. He cleared his throat, his eyes darting back and forth as if considering some hidden question. Had he really not known about Elijah's death? Sophie paused. Cash's claims were obviously untrue, she had caught him red-handed, and Marie had no reason to lie to her. The grief was real. Marie earnestly believed her brother had gone to meet Cash earlier that same day.

Slowly, with confidence so manufactured Sophie felt like she was watching a kindergarten play, Cash replied, "Listen, that's awful. And I'm sorry to hear about this... this, uh, Lambert, kid. He must have gone to see someone else or got confused. Like I said, I've never heard of him."

To Sophie's eye, Cash Calloway seemed the sort of man used to exploiting 'the benefit of the doubt.' A smirk ticked at the corner of his mouth, a look Sophie had learned to pick out at a glance. Any audience member who gave her that look would never make it to her stage. Duper's Delight some performers called it. The smile of someone who thinks they've got you fooled.

But this wasn't a stage, and Sophie couldn't simply ignore the man. She'd just have to play her own games.

Sophie steepled her fingers, shaking her head in disappointment. Then, reaching into her suit coat, Sophie passed by the lockpicks and the deck of cards she kept on hand and pulled a delicate brass chain.

Cash tensed, and for a moment, Sophie was sure the man thought she was going to pull a gun on him. His posture turned to confusion as she finished fishing out a circular, clasped pocketwatch.

"What's that?" he asked.

Sophie ignored him, opening the watch and pretending to check the time as the ticking began to click by in a steady cadence. She let the rhythm roll, the level metronome pace lulling Cash Callaway, pulling his subconscious focus.

In that moment, she turned and looked out over the water. Reflexively, Cash turned to follow her look.

"You see him." Halfway between a statement and a question, Sophie kept her voice level, authoritative. She told him there was something to see, and so his mind would fill in the gaps. To see what she did.

And what did an alligator poacher expect to see, in the middle of the night, on the bayou?

Gators.

Letting the ticking pocket watch run, Sophie gingerly picked up the bait bucket. She didn't toss any pieces into the water. The plop could break the hypnotic effect her voice and the pocket watch were weaving.

Instead, with a soft underhand, she threw a slab of raw chuck onto Cash's chest.

He started, quickly pushing the meat off his shirt, looking at the stain left behind. "What're you doing?"

Sophie dropped another piece on Cash's prone body. And another.

"Stop that!" Cash called out, looking anxiously between Sophie and the dark water around them. "Stop!" He threw up his hands defensively but couldn't stand or reach her. "I don't know what happened to the little creep! He never showed up ok. He was supposed to meet me, but he never showed!"

Sophie upended the bait bucket, the rest of the chopped chicken and beef spilling out with a slime of grease and juice that soaked into Cash's clothes immediately.

"Tick tock, Cash," Sophie said calmly.

"I swear that's all I know!" he choked, his voice raw and wild now.

Sophie didn't look into the bayou. As far as poaching locations went, Cash had chosen a spot as likely to have alligators as Toronto. Looking at the condition of the stagnant run, she'd have been surprised if they found any fish, let alone gators big enough to be worth the trouble.

But as long as Cash believed it, every log and floating branch became a fresh source of terror for him.

"Alright!" Cash shouted. "I saw him, ok?"

Bingo. Sophie folded her arms, casually turning the ticking pocket watch between her fingers. "What happened when you met with him?"

Cash shuddered, curling up under the lip of the airboat's hull. "There was this guy. He met me a few days ago. Said he knew what I did. About the poaching, I mean."

"What guy?" Sophie interjected. "Did you know him?"

"No." Cash shook his head violently. "He was wearing this, this—hood, I guess? Like a Halloween mask. One of those dark ones with no eyes or mouth. He wore it under a baseball cap, like it was nothing."

"What did he want?"

Pulling at the collar of his t-shirt, Cash said, "He wanted to give me money. Like a whole fistful of money. Said he knew I was meeting the kid—"

"Elijah?"

"Yeah," Cash pointed up at Sophie. "Yeah, he knew we were meeting and he said to take the kid to this place out by the river. That there would be a van there. All I had to do was get the kid in the van, and he said he'd do the rest."

"A van?" Sophie felt her heart twist. "What kind of van?"

Cash shook his head again, Sophie could see the sheen of sweat beading on his forehead as his voice began to tumble in an anxious jumble.

"Look, I don't know. Just like, a work van, y'know? Big double doors in the back. White. No windows except in the front. Just a work van. I didn't know he was gonna kill him, I swear!"

"What did you think he was going to do, Cash?" Sophie snapped. All desire to keep up the hypnotic effect had disappeared, replaced by fury. This man might not have killed Elijah Lambert, but if what he was saying was true, he may as well have.

His palms came up in a pleading gesture as bait rolled off his neck and slopped off his arms and legs. "Look, I told you all I know, now get me outta here! You can't feed me to the gators, man! C'mon. It ain't right. It ain't right!"

Sophie wondered for a brief moment how true that statement really was. A brutal, indulgent anger boiled in her chest as she imagined what sort of fate a man like Cash Calloway deserved.

Then, taking a deep breath, she released the feeling. He would go to the police. She would see him arrested for his involvement, at bare minimum, held for the poaching while they investigated.

This wasn't about revenge, she reminded herself. But behind the thought, the figure of a man in a baseball cap, a tattoo on his upper arm, appeared. In her imagination, the figure lifted a black, fabric Halloween mask just high enough to bite a cigar and light it.

Sophie clicked the pocket watch closed, nipping the inside of her cheek as she refocused. Cash Calloway had sold a young man to the killer for no more than a thousand dollars. But why? Why would the killer hire a local to kidnap Elijah? Why didn't the killer do it himself?

There was something there, and as Sophie spun up the airboat's fan and turned to follow the river back into Peillon, she muttered to herself, "RK, what are you doing?"

Chapter 16

The satisfaction was ecstasy. The murderer ran his fingers over the pages of his notebook, his fingertips sensitive to the slick, black lines of the ink and the scent of the crackling paper as he tenderly turned each leaf.

He looked out of the window of the van, his eyes tearing up as they drank in the crescent of clear moon above the suburban neighborhood.

"If I have seen so far, it is because I have stood on the shoulders of giants," he whispered, and a fresh shudder ran through his body.

Two brilliant performances.

Rolling back through the book, he reached a stiff page, double thick from glue and cut newspaper. His own scrawling handwriting filled the narrow space around the article, but he only had eyes for the newsprinted face glaring out at him. He pulled the fold of the notebook over his nose and laid a tender kiss over the page.

"Thank you, Hoffrey," he croaked over the faded image of the Butcher of Memphis. Turning to another stiff page, he bowed his head. "And to you, cher, my beautiful river spirit. To all of you."

Guilt panged in his heart and the page crinkled as his fingers reflexively curled.

He had nearly messed up. His second performance had gone well, but he had nearly lost the young man. All his preparation almost gone to waste. He had adjusted, corrected the schedule and made sure the rich, young man was where he needed him to be, but even then...

His hand drifted to his chest, feeling where he'd been kicked in the chest.

"Stupid," he chided himself. "Stupid. Stupid. Stupid. Stupid." With each pass, his hand clenched deeper into a fist, striking at his own chest.

He would do better. He would do much better.

The murderer pocketed his notebook, pulling his cap low over his eyes. He did not need to look at the dark house as he approached. He had rehearsed.

No dogs. No alarms. A chain and bolt on both the front and back door, but as he had seen already, his latest victim never seemed to remember the bolt in the back.

The satchel at his hip held a bottle of chloroform, still more than halfway filled. A few rags as well, the lingering odor of the chemical kept at bay by the bag's zipper. But beyond that?

He smiled as he flicked the rubber band between his fingers, the small, bass thrum delighting him as he opened the back door the first few inches. As expected, the chain rattled from the dark interior, but he had practiced this as well.

With one hand, the murderer slipped the band around the nub of the chain in its slot. Careful not to lose his grip, he stretched the band down, looping it on the edge of the door handle below. Tight, well-connected on both ends.

Retreating his hand back out through the three-inch gap in the door, he held his breath, listening for one moment for any sound of movement. He was certain they would be well asleep by now, but one could never be too careful. Then, he closed the door.

Tension released, the rubber band shrank, and the murderer listened to the slip and clack of the chain as it dropped from its slot. A gentle tap on the tile within as the rubber band fell free.

The next push of the door swung fully and silently open. A master couldn't have done it better, he thought.

And that was what he would be.

A master. His deeds etched in fear and urban legend for generations to come.

Just one more performance. One more emulation. Even Da Vinci practiced by copying those who came before him.

He crept through the house, feeling his way in total darkness. He had been here before. In daytime. He had practiced different routes, chosen this path to the stairs. He knew which steps creaked and which sections of the handrail sagged. And as he came to the bedroom door, he found it open.

Just as he had the week before and the week before that.

A sigh. He watched the sleepers' chest rise and fall. They were alone, face up, their covers pushed down to their ankles against the summer heat.

The faintest hiss of the satchel's zipper was lost under the hum of the ceiling fan, and the scent of chloroform followed the softly whirling currents of air.

One more performance. One more mile in the shoes of his predecessors.

The murderer smiled and crossed the doorway.

Chapter 17

Sophie rubbed her eye with the heel of her hand. If she'd accompanied the Peillon PD as they carted away Cash Calloway, she probably could have made use of their bathroom sink to exorcise the smell of gator bait from her fingers.

But it was nearly 2 AM and her body craved a hot shower and sleep so, with her statement given, she made sure the locals had her number and made a sleepy beeline for the grime-faded sign that marked the Creek Bed Motel.

She didn't need to look at the phone again. She remembered the motel's location from her childhood, and her mind had locked in the room number Greer had sent her immediately. Still, she had made it halfway between the sedan and her door, her overnight bag in hand, before she remembered she hadn't picked up her key from the front desk. The late-night clerk only grunted as he handed over her key, deciding a proper greeting wasn't worth the effort to pull his eyes away from the video playing on his phone. Not that Sophie was eager for conversation.

No. Sleep. Stepping back across the parking lot to the row of room doors, sleep was all she wanted.

"Thought you might have stolen it."

Sophie started, one heel sliding back as her hands came up in a boxer's stance, her room key gripped like a dagger, her back against the exterior wall of the motel.

"Whoa! Easy." The voice was smooth, with just a hint of roughness at the back, almost like a late-night radio host.

"Greer. I didn't see you there," Sophie said, relaxing her stance and falling with one shoulder against her room door. "What are you doing up?"

Tall and fit, Agent Jonathan Greer stood a few doors down, holding a comically small bucket in one hand as he gestured to the ice machine tucked into the motel's wall. "Ice," he replied simply.

For a moment, Sophie could only stare. She'd seen Greer in his neatly fitted suit and swimming in baggy clothes taken from her father after their canal chase, but now he stood in a pair of loose-fitting pajama bottoms and a tight-fitting undershirt, a white t-shirt that caught every curve and shadow from the dim porch-lighting of the motel's canopy roof.

She had suspected the ex-marine engineer kept himself in good shape. Now the evidence was undeniable, as even the simple gesture to the ice machine showed an arm med students could have used to practice their anatomy. Not that he was bulky, no, the definition Sophie saw was lean, practical muscle.

Why am I thinking about his arm? Sophie could feel exhaustion muddling her mind.

Greer seemed to take Sophie's lingering stare for disbelief, because after a quick cough, he began to pass the bucket back and forth between his hands. "I couldn't sleep," he amended. "And I was joking... before?"

"Huh?" Sophie looked up into Greer's eyes, the strikingly pale blue meeting hers for only a moment before looking away into the parking lot.

"I didn't actually think you stole it," he gestured to the white sedan. "My car, I mean."

"Oh," Sophie cracked a grin and ran a hand through her short shock of hair. "I'm sorry... if I kept you up."

"Oh, no. Nothing like that," Greer shook his head with a short chopping wave of his hand. "I just have trouble sleeping sometimes. You know, it's funny. I had all these tricks when I was in the Marines. I've slept while listening to artillery shelling a position not five miles from us. But it feels like, anymore, the quiet gets to me."

Sophie sighed. She imagined that she must look as tired as he did. Maybe even more. But the athletic agent's fidgeting, his inability to keep his hands or his eyes still... He was thinking something. Something he didn't feel comfortable saying out loud. And for just a moment, the grey shot through his hair gave him a haunted appearance.

The night brings that out in us all, I suppose, Sophie thought. She wondered if Agent Greer had any skeletons in his closet. Perhaps that was why they had ended up partnered together. Two lost souls working a case with no sane answer. Fate was funny that way. Not that Sophie believed in fate. Not for the good things in life anyway.

She gave Greer a reassuring wink, tilting the side of her head against the doorframe. Her voice was gentle, respecting the hour. "An old friend of mine used to say 'If you can't sleep. Practice'."

Greer nodded thoughtfully. "That's good advice. Is that how you ended up famous?"

Sophie shrugged. "I'm certainly not the first woman to ever have a magic act."

"Is that why you're still up tonight? Can't sleep?"

Sophie paused for a moment. Greer had stopped fidgeting when he asked the question. He wasn't avoiding her look anymore.

There were times being a mentalist and a hypnotist showed her more than she wanted to see. People couldn't help themselves, especially when they were off guard. Tired. Angry. Scared. Their bodies betrayed them. Sophie sighed through her lips.

"That's not what you want to ask me," she said, her disappointment carrying the words on the final edge of her breath. "You want to ask where I was. You're just too polite to say it. Am I wrong?"

Greer stiffened, just a little. But it was too late. He knew he'd been seen. He nodded.

Sophie returned the gesture. "I followed up on Elijah Lambert. I found out who he was supposed to see today. A man named Cash Calloway. I followed him out into the bayou and got his confession. He helped kidnap the victim. He spoke with the killer... Peillon PD have him in a holding cell, and we can interview him tomorrow."

Greer's jaw dropped. He looked from Sophie to the ice machine and then back to the empty bucket in his hands. "Why didn't you call me? We could have gone together." His strong shoulders bunched. His jaw shifted as if chewing on his tongue. "We agreed, remember? I don't keep anything from you, you don't keep anything from me."

Sophie clicked her tongue, looking back to the drizzling rain glistening in the parking lot beside them. "I remember. I remember you telling me that I deserved to be on this case. That you wanted to help me solve it. But... are we even on the same case anymore? You don't even think this is RK."

"Someone is killing these people, Quinn. Maybe it's RK, maybe it's not," Greer threw up a hand, jabbing a finger towards his chest. "I have to follow the evidence. I'm not about to let some other lunatic get away because you're trying to shoehorn every clue back to your own personal boogeyman."

A rush of cold ran down Sophie's spine. She couldn't do this. Not now. They were both exhausted and continuing to argue wasn't going to change that. Turning her back on Greer, the big man started to say, "Hold on a moment—" as Sophie unlocked the motel door and stepped through.

"Goodnight, Agent Greer."

As she locked the door, Sophie saw the vague shape of the tall agent silhouetted against the blinds. A few seconds passed, and then that was gone too.

Sophie closed her eyes, talking herself through a brief and shallow level of self-hypnosis, calming herself. Releasing the anger boiling in her chest. Once she finished, she set to the arcane task of finding the perfect temperature in the motel shower.

She tried to organize her thoughts, to break down the evidence and to picture RK behind it all. A black mask under a baseball cap. Despite herself, as her muscles relaxed and the grime and sweat of the day made their way down the drain, she thought back to her parents.

Her mama's face, the hurt and disappointment in her daddy's voice. They had been so happy to see her. Genuinely... happy. Six years she'd stayed away. Six years, she could only think of how bitter she'd been the last time they'd been together. How could they be so... cheerful? So at peace?

They aren't, her inner voice countered. You saw what happened. As soon as you brought reality into the picture, RK, Molly, the new murders, they crumbled.

And yet, they were surrounded by people. Laughter. Community.

Who do you have, Sophie Quinn?

Jus' you and me, eh, cher? A match made in heaven, the cancerous laugh, RK's coarse, cigar-bitten voice drove all other thoughts from her mind.

Sophie flung the valve completely to cold. The showerhead sputtered as icy water shocked her bare back and sent a shiver of gooseflesh over her. And for a count of twenty, Sophie thought only about the freezing sensation spreading through her.

Later, lying in bed, a hotel robe between her and the comforter, Sophie fished around in her overnight bag. The last time she'd wanted to run away from home this bad, she'd been apprenticed to the Great Gavriel. She smiled, thinking of the cranky, old Bostonian.

Something rattled in her bag, a string of beads, too few colors to make a rainbow but too many for any sane pattern. Some bright and pastel, others opaque and matte as cloth. Seashell designs, flowers, geometric angles and soft spirals. The bracelet held no rhyme or reason to justify the cacophony of charms strung along its well-worn, leather strap.

If she thought about it, Sophie could trace back every one to a letter Gavriel had sent her. From the very first, a clay sunflower in creamy acrylic yellow to the latest, a starburst of black and crimson with glossy coating she could see her eyes in. From the first week off the bus in LA to her apartment in Detroit. Ron Gavriel never forgot her. *What Would Gavriel Do,* she mused to herself, slipping the chaotic chain of beads around her wrist.

A part of her wanted to give her old teacher a call. Being raised by parents who never acknowledged a problem, the old magician's ability to break down and solve the trouble that came their way was practically a magic trick in itself; and usually done with whatever was on hand, *I'm not made-a money after all...*

Sophie toyed with her phone another moment. It was too late to call. Far too late. She should be asleep herself, but despite her shower and all her efforts to relax, Sophie felt her mind continuing to turn on its own.

Who would copy the River Killer? And the Memphis Butcher's style too? Why now? Was it really a copycat? It bothered Sophie that she couldn't see what others seemed to; how murky the boundary to obsession really could be. She was determined, that's what she was feeling. Wasn't it?

Sophie picked at the beads, turning them thoughtfully.

"Well, kid," she murmured to herself, picking up the deck of cards from her suit coat. "If you can't sleep. Practice."

Chapter 18

Greer passed a hot, styrofoam cup of coffee to Sophie. Beyond a question of whether she took cream or sugar with her brew—a splash of cream, no sweetener—the pair hadn't shared more than a half-dozen words that morning. In a fresh but equally tan suit, Greer grimaced and Sophie guessed he also tasted the few free-floating grounds that the local PD's coffee machine had let through.

"Do you think he really doesn't know who paid him for the kidnapping?" Greer asked, appraising the grainy image on the ten-inch monitor in front of them. On it, the forty-four-year-old man handcuffed to the steel table hunched forward, apparently attempting to scratch—no, pick—at his nose.

Sophie took another sip, she was running on perhaps four hours of sleep, but she trusted the caffeine would catch her up. She had performed in worse conditions.

"He never saw a face," Sophie answered. "He was terrified, in no state to make up a whole line about a Halloween mask. He admitted he saw the van and what he was paid to do, so why lie about that?"

"Could be scared," Greer replied. "Afraid the guy who hired him will come back and kill him too?"

Sophie let out a quick scoff. "Not more afraid than he was of me."

Greer frowned, "The tread at Gatlin Park was inconclusive," he added. "It might be the same van that was outside Demi Wilson and Hazel Michel's hotel room. But we can't prove it."

"Still more likely than two unconnected killers with their own vans."

Greer grunted in agreement. "So what else are we looking for?"

Sophie didn't know. They could start combing the DMV for every record of a work van from here to New Orleans, but by the time they followed up on those leads, more people would already be dead. No, the way forward was through Cash Calloway. He had to know something, to have seen something... even if he didn't know it yet.

Shrugging as she took one last pull from her coffee cup, Sophie headed to the hallway door. "Let's find out."

The interrogation room at the Peillon Police Department smelled like mildew. The camera staring down at Cash Calloway's scraggly beard fed a wire behind the one-way glass into the dark room with the single CRT monitor attached to a hard drive twenty years its junior.

His head popped up as the pair of investigators entered, and he gave a choking, phlegmatic cough as he spied Sophie.

"Oh, what now?" Cash whined, his head lolling as he slouched back in the metal chair.

"Mr. Calloway," Greer said, direct and clear, "Last night you told my partner that you were paid by a man in a dark mask and baseball cap to kidnap Elijah Lambert."

"I didn't kidnap anybody!" Cash said with a tremble. "I just brought him to a van. I made sure he got in the van, that's all! Getting in a car ain't kidnapping."

Sophie took a seat, tapping the table with a fingertip. "Well, it wasn't a date, Cash."

He threw a glare Sophie's way, and by the sudden set of his jaw, she was certain he had bit back some insult.

Keeping her own face passive, Sophie continued, "Look, people have struck deals for less. I'm not here to try and put you away on kidnapping or poaching or any of that. Someone is out here killing people. Methodically. Cruelly. It's a game to them. A game they absolutely will not stop until they are caught. You didn't know what this guy wanted to do with Elijah? Fine. Have it your way. But give us something... anything."

Greer joined in, turning his hands like he was wrapping a ball of yarn between them. "A scar? A tattoo? Did the van have any decals or bumper stickers?"

Cash's mouth drew into a tight line, his eyes ticked between anger and exhaustion. "I don't know. I only saw him once! He met me at my home, told me what to do. I only caught a glimpse of him when he dropped the money out of the van after, but never his face. I swear to God."

Fear. Entirely selfish fear, but it was seeping out of every pore on his face.

Sophie realized then what had happened. He'd been pushed to the edge. He couldn't think straight, couldn't remember anything because he was still riding the terror from the night before. Add to this the fear that she could see flaring up every time the killer was mentioned, and Sophie saw a man too obsessed with how to save his own life to look into the face of the monster. To remember what happened, calmly and clearly.

Tapping Greer on the shoulder, Sophie stood and retreated to the corner of the room. As he followed, Greer spoke in a low whisper.

"His story isn't changing. You want to turn up the heat? Good cop, bad cop?"

Sophie shook her head sharply. "That'll only close him up more."

"What then?"

"I have an idea," Sophie said. "But you're not going to like it."

Greer glanced at the camera in the corner of the room and rubbed at his neck thoughtfully. "Try me."

Taking a quick breath, Sophie said, "I want to hypnotize him."

Greer immediately tilted his head, looking from the one-way glass back to Sophie. "The lawyers will have a field day if we try to bring in hypnotized testimony."

"I know that," Sophie said, tapping her palm on Greer's chest. "I know how it looks. If you can get someone to stand on one leg and cluck like a chicken, you can get them to confess to murder. Even murders they didn't do. I know how that goes, but that's not what I'm saying."

"What's the play then?"

"I calm him down. Get him to think clearly. He has to have seen something, even if he didn't realize it." Sophie ran her tongue along her teeth, waiting for Greer's answer.

If this went badly, they'd be worse off than having no clues at all. False memories were a risk even under the best conditions, it was only a matter of time before Calloway became desperate enough to start making things up. But as long as she was careful...

"This is going to look bad," the tall agent said.

Sophie followed Greer's gaze to the room's camera. He was right. This could end both of their careers if that recording made it to the right hands. There was no reason for him to go down with her though.

"You can step out," Sophie said. "Get some coffee. Say you didn't know what I was going to do."

Greer's blue eyes locked with hers, the cracks at the corners of his dark lashes contracting with focus. It was an intense stare. Deep. Probing. Then with a quick click of his tongue, Greer seemed to reach a decision. "I'll take care of the camera. You have five, maybe ten minutes at most." And on the final word, he stepped through the door, back into the hallway.

Sophie knew he had technical skills. Her experience with cameras ended at the lens, but if Greer said he could disable it, she believed him. But would he? There were times the man had been frustratingly difficult to read...

The blinking red of the ancient security camera's recording light didn't waver as Sophie took her seat again. It continued as she reached into her pocket and took out her brass pocket watch, opening the clasp and setting it on the table between her and Calloway.

She took a deep breath.

"What are you doing?" Cash asked, glancing between Sophie and the open pocket watch.

She knew his eyes would be drawn to the metronome tick of the second hand as it circled the watch face. She let the sound and the sight do their work, relaxing in her seat, silently inviting Cash to do the same.

"We're going to slow down," she said. "We both need to take a breath." Sophie took a long breath, and despite the mistrust still in his eyes, Cash Calloway subconsciously did the same.

Sophie looked into his eyes, her soft voice supported by the tick of the pocket watch. "Just a breath. We're safe here. Just talking. Looking without judgment. Like turning through the pictures in a photo album."

Cash's shoulders relaxed. He drooped in his chair, exhaustion and hypnotic suggestion working in tandem on his weary mind. Too intimidated to look Sophie in the eye, his gaze returned again and again to the steady climb of the small hands on the pocket watch.

Sophie didn't look over her shoulder, didn't check if the light in the camera had gone dark. A momentary image flicked in her mind of Merchant and Meyer, both field offices merged in a brief instant of anxiety as they threw her out, her consultation contract revoked, tapes of this interrogation played at a federal hearing.

She inhaled.

Alright, Greer, I'm trusting you...

"Close your eyes. We're back at your cabin. Safe. Alone."

Lulled by the slow build of Sophie's voice and the steady rhythm of the pocket watch, Cash Calloway closed his eyes. His nose whistled, his stomach muscles relaxed, and his palms lay flat on the table.

"You were here when you met a masked man," Sophie stated, gently, simply. "What do you hear?"

Calloway licked his lips, a flicker of worry creasing his eyebrows. His breathing shifted, picking up, but only a little.

"Gravel. Tires on the dirt road. Footsteps. Boots, crunching. I'm by the dock and I'm finishing tying off my boat."

"What do you see?" Sophie prompted. She didn't mention the killer or the van. She didn't want to lead his thinking, didn't want to prompt memories that weren't there...

"His face is covered. I get a grip on my pocket knife, just in case. But he doesn't move fast," Calloway takes a sucking breath, a hiss between his teeth. "He shows me the cash. He's not big... but he sounds... rough. Solid. He sounds like my grandad. Chew and pipe."

An older man. That made sense. Sophie fought back her own memories of RK's graveled voice, using her own pocket watch to wrangle her thoughts back to the moment. "What happens next?"

"We talk," Cash says, his voice tighter now.

"It's alright, Cash. You're safe. What happens after you talk?"

There's a small tremble in Cash's voice. "We talk about Elijah... where to bring him. He asks if I have a gun..."

Sophie's neck tensed. He was starting to spiral, fear and the edges of buried guilt beginning to bubble up. She needed to cut him off before he broke. But they couldn't stop. He had to know something!

Leaning forward, Sophie dropped her voice, no note of hurry or anxiety allowed to creep in. She had to keep him calm. "He's leaving now. The masked man is leaving... what do you see?"

Cash nods. "He's walking to the road. Back to his car."

Sophie bit her own lip to stop herself from asking if he meant a van. Instead, she asked, "What does his car look like?"

"Blue. Like a girl's car. Like Easter. It's strange. Squat... little. It even has these 'mini' wings." Cash gave an anxious chuckle. "Must be New Orleans. I never heard an engine like that. Like a wasp flying by your ear."

Sophie felt her heart beginning to race. A second car? Did that make sense? She could think of a few reasons why a killer might use different vehicles, but this was the first they'd heard of it. She knew she shouldn't lead the memory, but if this was all they had...

"Cash. What does the license plate say?"

The bearded man's eyes squinched together like he was squinting behind his eyelids. "I can't see it..."

"Please," Sophie asked, a slight urgency creeping into her voice. "He turned past you. You saw the plates." She was playing with fire now. If Cash really didn't see the plates, his highly suggestible mind might make up a detail just to fill in the gaps.

Cash's lip trembled, his head subtly tipping forward. "Louisiana... Pray... Pray... I didn't see the numbers, but... pray. P. R. Y." Suddenly, Cash's hands went wide. His body stiffened. "He's here," he said. "He knows what I said."

Sophie slapped her hand down on the pocket watch. Cash started, his eyes blinking rapidly like he was waking from a dream. "What did you do to me?"

The ticking buried by her hand, she slipped the watch back into her coat. "You need more sleep, Mr. Calloway," she said, calmly, turning and striding for the door. Her mind racing over the new details.

A blue car...

And a prayer.

Chapter 19

The snap of Greer's fingers from across the hall cut her off before Sophie could say a word. Her back tensing, she was about to tell the blue-eyed agent exactly what she thought of being snapped at when she heard the approaching footsteps and jangle of Peillon's finest coming to check on their poacher. With a jerk of his chin, Greer indicated the empty break room, turning to intercept the officers.

A moment later, he joined her.

"I told them Cash needs more sleep," Greer said, looking out through the break room window as the officers marched Calloway back to the holding cells. "Just like you said. He's out of it and talking a bit crazy."

Sophie's stomach twisted at the comment, and the hum of the vending machines along with the smell of stale coffee left over from the morning shift change certainly didn't help.

"You heard that?"

He nodded, setting their laptop bags on the round plastic table beside the iron-barred window facing the station's rear parking lot. "Frankly, I'm a bit stunned. I didn't know what you'd be able to get out of him. A car, with a partial plate on top?" He let out a slow whistle.

"So the camera was rolling the whole time," Sophie said, her mouth drawn to the side in a hard line.

Greer looked up from his laptop, realization hitting him. "No. No, no, no, you're fine, Miss Quinn," he said, shooting a glance to the hallway. "I corrupted the recording routine. The camera software was running and I was listening in, but the system only recorded static."

Sophie's jaw dropped. But she gathered her wits enough to ask, "How did you manage that?" as she pulled out a hard plastic chair opposite Greer.

The ex-marine smirked. "I told you I was a Marine engineer. War has changed, Miss Quinn. I spent as much time blowing up spyware and dark web scraper sites as I did breaking down vehicles and convoy bridges. You could think of it like a double PhD, if you like." He capped off this last comment with a cheeky wink, and Sophie couldn't help but give a tired laugh back.

"Well, look at us," Sophie said, booting up her own laptop, "a couple of overachievers." Then, her smile fading, she added, "Thank you. You didn't have to do that."

Greer sighed, looking Sophie up and down. For just a moment, Sophie felt like she was back in LA, auditioning for a spot in that month's lineup. But there was no condescension in his expression. Only expectation.

"You're right. Nobody has to do anything. But that's not the point. We don't do what we do because it's expected or because it's the easy thing to do," Greer rubbed his eyes. "Look, I think you're trying to do the right thing. And I think you're used to getting hurt trying to do it. I get it... I think. Just..." His lips pursed, and Greer seemed on the verge of launching into some dramatic monologue. Instead, he simply said, "You don't always have to fall on your sword to do the right thing. Sometimes people really are here to help you out."

Determined people bleed for what they want. The obsessed make everyone else bleed for it.

Sophie didn't know if she believed the athletic agent. But he believed it. The steadiness in his voice and the unaffected attention he gave her as he spoke. Honesty. Maybe a hint of embarrassment.

"Thank you," Sophie said, quietly, almost shyly. Then she coughed, mouthing a quick apology as she looked down at her laptop and tried to suppress the color rising in her cheeks.

"So," she said, breaking the moment's grip on them, "Some sort of little, Easter-blue colored car. What are we thinking? Like a two-door sports car?"

Greer shook his head, his fingers sweeping across the laptop as he spoke. "No. He mentioned an electric whine. Said it was a bit squat too. I'm guessing, from that and a few other details, we have a powder-blue Mini Cooper on our hands."

"'Mini wings'," Sophie added, recalling Cash's hypnotized commentary.

"Exactly," Greer said, accenting the comment with a punch on the laptop. "Not exactly what leaps to mind when you think of a serial killer. But unique enough that when we pair it with the partial plate—" Another quick series of taps.

Spinning his laptop, Greer announced, "We get one Andrew Kelly."

Sophie punched the name into her own laptop as Greer turned his screen back around.

"He looks a bit lanky," she said, cautiously.

Greer shrugged. "His license photo is almost four years old. Maybe he's been working out?"

"Cash did say he was short," Sophie added.

"Five-foot-four. Shorter than Cash," Greer admitted.

Sophie scanned the page of results on her screen, clicking through general web-links and references. "Hold on, he has a true crime blog."

A black and red webpage loaded in front of her. Dripping blood fonts and low-resolution pictures accompanied the banner and archive listings. If any website could look 'homemade' Andrew Kelly's *Blood Inked Confessionals* certainly fit the bill.

"Confessions?" Greer asked, trepidation in his voice as he leaned over to peek at Sophie's screen.

"No, I don't think so anyway. The titles are what you'd expect from an ordinary true crime site. He's been at this a while though. There are hundreds of them. Hold on. His most recent, a week ago."

"What is it?"

Sophie glanced up, her expression grim. "Hoffrey Timms."

Greer sat back. Both of them, no doubt, thinking of Elijah Lambert's suspended body, killed the same way the Memphis Butcher, Hoffrey Timms, had slain his victims.

Sophie's eyes went wide as she mouthed the words on her screen. "Oh, God," she murmured.

Greer stood, rounding the table as Sophie began to read the blog post aloud.

"*I pull the rope taut. He's hanging now, like a Christmas turkey trussed up in the window. The knife in my hand catches the moonlight as I raise it. I must be quick, precise. One cut across the throat...*"

Greer's brow furrowed as he put a palm on the table beside Sophie. "What the hell..."

"He's writing it from the killer's point of view," Sophie explained. "Like he was the one doing it."

The implication hung heavy in the air as Greer returned to his own laptop. "Serial killers go through stages," he started to explain. "Stage one, fantasy."

Sophie continued the thought. "But the fantasy isn't enough. Then they role play, acting it out. Finally, when pretending just isn't enough anymore..."

Greer's laptop chirped and he swung back around to the newly loaded page. "He's renting a place in Curting. Change of address dated back a week ago."

Sophie stood abruptly. "That's only fifteen minutes from here."

"Hold up a moment," Greer said, raising a palm.

"We don't have time," Sophie answered, shouldering her laptop bag.

"We're not driving out to a serial killer's house without being prepared," Greer answered firmly. "Merchant cleared you for open carry."

"She did?"

Greer nodded. "You should have an agency car in the lot too if you feel the need to split up again. Not that Merchant was keen about the idea."

"Greer," Sophie interrupted, motioning to the door.

"Right. Let's just get you holstered up, *then* we'll go take down this sicko. Deal?"

"Deal."

As the pair reached their car, Sophie looked up into the dawn light. Three deaths in two days. The last victim died in the late afternoon. She tried not to focus on how many hours they may have until the next victim.

But she could not stop thinking through the hundreds of killers listed in Andrew Kelly's blog, or which fantasy he could choose for his next re-enactment.

Chapter 20

The pink dawn called to him like rose petals on a nuptial bed. There had been rain the night before, and he had worried the inconstant weathermen would foul up his plans. It would not have been the first time. But here he was, humming along the southbound highway, a bright and beautiful day before him.

A day of promise.

His final tribute.

The murderer fingered the notebook in his breast pocket. He didn't bother with GPS even though one was built right into the dashboard.

He knew exactly where he was going. Clipped pages from a road atlas, marked in yellow highlighter and black ink, were glued in beside his other notes: Her age; Her work schedule; When the lights on her kitchen went dark each night and the results of numerous tests on the locks and latches around her first floor.

He had driven this route several times, just as he had walked their destination until he could see it in his dreams.

A small groan rose from the seat beside him, and the murderer smiled. "Nearly there, darlin," he said, reaching over to pat his victim's knee. It would be another forty minutes at least, likely longer, but there was no harm in the lie. She would be unconscious for hours yet. But the jangle of the imperfect highway pavement would make it an uneasy sleep. He hoped the blanket and neck pillow he'd provided would keep her somewhat comfortable. The thought of their performance together being uglied by something as base as a stiff neck made him fidget with anxiety.

And there was plenty else to be anxious about.

The rain the night before concerned him. Sometimes people delayed their trips to parks and nature reserves over the clouds and the threat of rain. If all those people who meant to come the day before came today, it could be quite crowded on the trails. But no, he had intentionally scouted the most crowded days he could and his chosen location was still empty and discrete. Even if someone saw them, what would they see? Two lovers on a picnic in the shade of a flowering dogwood?

And would anyone question his stiff and groggy companion? No. He had dressed her for the occasion. She would stand out but only by the wheelchair he would use to walk her through the park. A sweet man and his sickly, young wife out to enjoy the summer sun while they can. Yes, that was what they would think.

After all, no one had given him strange looks or commented when he had done the same with a well-covered mannequin. No, not either time.

He had run the chair over rough ground and knew he would not get stuck. There would be no need for strangers to lend a hand. No wheel caught in the mud or sudden slip over a steep slope.

The man gazed lovingly to the dawn light then closed his eyes, letting the cruise control hurry him along the empty highway just a little further as he patted the notebook like a lucky charm.

"Thank you, Norman, for showing me the way. My final performance. The keys to my own kingdom yet to come," he muttered prayerfully. Yes. A lovely summer walk. A picnic. And then a swim.

Oh, how she would swim.

Chapter 21

"Only moving boxes in here too. Some old newspapers. Craft supplies." Sophie dropped a pair of scissors beside a glue stick on an empty desk.

Greer's ID had been enough for the landlord to let them into the rental home. No car in the driveway and no sign of Andrew Kelly beyond the boxes of clothing, mystery novels, and horror movies that showcased his recent move.

"Change of address from a week ago and he's still living out of boxes," Greer said dubiously, shifting a cardboard box that clattered with poorly wrapped kitchenware.

"He's been busy the last week," Sophie reminded her partner. "Maybe he hasn't had time to settle in," she said.

But the idea bothered her, and as Sophie cleared another room with no sign of where Kelly could be at eight o'clock on a Sunday morning, she realized why. The killer had been precise, well-prepared and methodical. Not the sort of person who wouldn't bother to take the time to unpack and organize their own home. Something wasn't right here.

She looked up as Greer joined her, his phone in hand.

"Anything?" he asked.

Sophie put a hand on her hip, shaking her head. "Nothing. How's the GPS tracking coming?"

Greer clicked his tongue in mock disappointment. "He has a bad connection. But we're picking up a ping from the other side of the highway."

"Is he running?" Sophie asked.

She couldn't help but feel a sharp urgency as they walked back to the car.

"No," he answered. "He's staying put. Looks like a residential address. Here." Greer passed the cellphone to Sophie as they pulled out of the rental home's driveway. "See what you can find out about that address. If he's going after someone who lives there we need to get in touch with them."

They ripped along the side roads leading out of Curting and through the wider avenues leading back to the highway. The trees gave way to broad marshes and long bridgeways cutting across ground too wet to ever support a stable road. Urgency seemed to drive the engine louder, or perhaps Sophie was just more aware of their speed as they broke around slower traffic, shattering the morning peace over dozens of neighborhoods.

The offshoots and bayou riverways feeding off the Mississippi made for beautiful scenery, and Sophie was reminded again of the crawdad boil her parents had hosted the other day. Small communities all up and down these rivers would be waking up, fishing, going to church. Licensed hunters would be checking traps or boating around with a few beers and baited hooks, hoping to catch a gator while the season was good. Later that day, in other suburbs and trailer parks, among loved ones and friends, people would gather for their own parties. Fish fries and hot pots.

Lives were being lived. A bit mud-scuffed, but living.

If her parents invited her again, would she go? Would it be another six years before she was welcome? The pain in the thoughts drove an explosive sigh from Sophie's nostrils.

"Find something?" Greer asked.

Sophie blinked, the question breaking her out of her thoughts. "Hold on, it's just loading." She plugged in the address Andrew Kelly's phone GPS was pinging from, running it through the FBI databases. "Oh, no."

"What is it?" Greer looked over to the phone, the car veering slightly as he split his attention.

"The address. I don't think it's a victim." Sophie scrolled through the file, her photographic memory drinking in the information as quickly as she saw it. "Geoff Tamer. Served thirty years for the murder of his girlfriend, Jessica Montgomery. He was just released two months ago."

Two cars, a van and a Mini Cooper. Was this another victim or an accomplice? Two killers would explain the divergence in methods. But if he already had an ally, why would Kelly hire Cash Calloway to kidnap his third victim? Sophie restlessly stretched her fingers as she set aside the questions. There would be no answers until they spoke with Kelly and Tamer.

The engine roared as Greer pushed the white agency car as hard as it would bear.

When they arrived, no words were necessary.

A navy blue work van, rusted along the wheel wells, sat beside a powder-blue Mini Cooper. The license plate's prominent lettering matching Andrew Kelly's registration.

The home was a single-story prefab. A front stoop led down from a battered screen door to a concrete walkway that ended abruptly at the gravel driveway feeding into the street. A rust-red weathervane sat beside an old satellite tv antenna as if they were shipped together in a set.

Despite the morning sun, interior lights shone through the rectangular windows, and the muffled sounds of voices made their way out in sporadic bursts of clarity, as if the speaker were moving around, speaking in every direction. One thin and soft, the other like sandpaper polishing a handful of marbles.

Greer gingerly closed the door, motioning for silence. They approached carefully, trying to listen while their athletic shoes rolled in soft heel-toe steps that kept the gravel driveway from grinding too loudly under them.

"Of course," the rougher voice exclaimed from inside the house. "You feel powerful... sick. Sorta like you're not human anymore. Like you're something else."

Sophie glanced to Greer's hands. He drew his pistol, holding it towards the ground in both hands while he side-stepped up to the front door. Sophie did the same. Crowded together on the stoop, the wood moaning underfoot in spite of their care, they flanked the screen door. Opening it carefully, propping it behind Greer's back. He tested the latch on the front door.

It was unlocked.

The softer voice spoke, too low to be heard, but the rough voice answered. "Exactly. Like there are two kinds of people—"

Greer looked from Sophie to the door handle. With one hand gesturing to support his words, he whispered, "On three. One."

"Two kinds. Killers and bleeders. And you... "

"Two."

"—You're a killer now."

"Three."

Greer raised his gun, shouldering through the door at the same moment. "FBI! On the ground, on the ground, now!"

Rushing in behind the tall agent, Sophie caught sight of the two men. One was thin and short, with the presence and bearing of a broken broom shoved in a corner closet. He sat at a kitchen table the size of a pizza box, his eyes wide and spread, looking like a chameleon behind glasses too thick for anything but heavy plastic frames. Sophie recognized him immediately. Andrew Kelly, true crime blogger.

The second figure was on his feet, pacing the room in work boots and a worn pair of jeans. He wasn't wearing a shirt and in addition to being as tall as Greer, appeared to top three-hundred pounds. His bare physique showed sloping muscle across his shoulders and arms that heavy layers of hair and fat only barely obscured. As soon as Greer turned to face the enormous man, he flicked a cigarette from his mouth, letting it hit the beige linoleum flowers that covered his small kitchen's floor.

Greer continued to shout, "Hands up! On the ground, now!" But the larger man, who must have been Geoff Tamer, snarled, an inarticulate shout of his own shooting back. And like a fighting dog, he leapt, hands and teeth first, for the agent.

Instead of a gunshot, broken mugs crashed as Tamer shoved Greer back against the kitchen cabinets. The big man's hand moved from Greer's chest to his throat. His other paw reached for the gun as Greer dropped his shoulder and pulled the weapon out of reach.

Andrew Kelly bolted to his feet, but Sophie stepped forward, her barrel trained on the scrawny man's *Friday the 13th* t-shirt. "Sit down," she snapped. Sophie threw her stage voice behind the command, a near-perfect copy of her partner's tone. Andrew Kelly immediately sat with his hands folded.

Greer's knee shot up, driving into Tamer's exposed stomach and sending a pained wheeze out of the man. With a gasping surge, Geoff Tamer threw a wild punch like a clothesline sweeping for Greer's neck. The tall agent ducked the blow, reaching up and snatching the exposed wrist with one hand as he spun back to back with his attacker.

His movements were fast and fluid, years of practice distilled into a one-sided dance. And with eyes trained to catch the subtle sleight-of-hand behind card tricks and illusions, Sophie watched as time seemed to slow down for Greer. He hooked Tamer's ankle with his own, twisting as he dragged the captured wrist over his shoulder. Suddenly Tamer was falling, his free hand trying to catch him as his chest slapped the linoleum with a heavy *whump.* The held arm bent painfully behind his back, Greer pinned a knee over Tamer's spine and pressed the cold metal of his pistol against the bare skin.

"Freeze."

And the next moment, the only sound was the uncomfortable gurgling of Geoff Tamer as he tried to catch his breath against the sticky tile.

Sophie caught Greer's eye and the former marine winked, letting out a quick breath of his own. She hadn't been afraid for him, not exactly, it had all happened too quickly for fear. But seeing him now, the shattered mugs broken on the cupboard shelves where Tamer had shoved him to the wall, Sophie felt a small sense of relief.

"So... uh. FBI, huh?" The high, mousy voice belonged to Kelly. His hands still folded, Sophie could see his Adam's apple nervously bobbing in his thin, Gandhi-like throat. "W-wh-what can we do, uh, what can we do for you?"

Sophie eyed the man suspiciously. He kept still, but beside his hands, she now saw a cell phone and a black notebook. It had fallen closed, but a click-pen lay between the leaves like a bookmark. His nervous eyes, thin limbs, and squeaking voice did not scream 'killer' to her. But she remembered what she'd heard on the way in. Was it an act? Was this pair the killer they had been searching for?

"Andrew Kelly," Sophie started. "We've been looking for you."

"You have? Why?"

His eyebrow beetled. Blinking as he looked away. Small ticks ran through Sophie's mental checklist of body language.

Confusion.

No misdirection or feigned ignorance. A genuine lack of understanding.

Sophie frowned. "We're investigating a series of murders in the Peillon area. Three deaths."

Kelly's mouth gaped. "Really? Three?"

Greer shifted, keeping Tamer well contained but angling to look Kelly in the eye. "We went to your home. Looks like you haven't been around much, now we find you in the home of a convicted murderer, talking about how it feels to commit murder. Call us concerned."

Tamer moaned as if he might say something, but he still hadn't caught his breath. Kelly's piping voice whistled over the sound. "Hold on. I'm a blogger. I tell true crime stories on my website."

"We know," Sophie interrupted. "We've been on *Blood Inked Confessionals*."

Kelly's eyes lit up. "You have? Are you a fan? Does the FBI read my work?" His fingers started to jitter as if they wanted to pick up the notebook and could only barely restrain themselves. "I like to think I have an eye for behavioral psychology. Though, I never formally studied. The criminal mind is *fascinating* to me."

Sophie crossed her arms. If this was an act, it was one he had played before. His excitement and confusion blended authentically without diluting each other.

"Mr. Kelly, we're not *fans*, we're investigators. People are dying. Real people. Not characters in a story. Now, what are you and Mr. Tamer doing here?" On the final question, Sophie gestured to the phone and notebook.

Kelly looked down at them as if he'd never seen them before, then a flash of recognition rolled over him. "Oh, this? I'm interviewing Mr. Tamer. I wanted his perspective. You know I do my work in the perspective of the killers I study, but it's so difficult to meet with people on death row or-or stuck away in maximum security like mummies locked away in a museum." As he spoke, the thin man's wide, lizard eyes pinched and narrowed with frustration. "Mr. Tamer has paid his due. He's been released and very graciously agreed to share his experiences with me."

"I'll bet," Greer said, his own expression going hard. "Mr. Kelly, I'm going to get straight to the chase. Those murders we mentioned, witnesses place a strong connection between them and a light blue Mini Cooper, as well as a large work van."

A pause lingered in the air, then Tamer suddenly shook under Greer's knee, his head whipping back and forth as he screamed, "I didn't do shit! You think just because I've got a record you can put this on me? I didn't do it."

Kelly was trembling now. His palms held up, he licked his lips. "Now hold on. I-I don't know what he may be involved with, I'm just here to do an interview. Maybe someone just saw me around town? Wait!" Nervously tapping at his cell phone, Kelly turned toward Sophie again. "You said the murders were recent? How recent? I mean, I just got here last week—"

"The murders were all within the last forty-eight to seventy-two hours," Greer said. Holstering his pistol, he slipped a pair of cuffs around Tamer's wrists while he spoke. "Plenty of time, particularly as you don't seem to have spent any of it unpacking your new home."

"Of course I didn't! I've been on vacation all week. I only just came back today because Mr. Tamer finally agreed to let me do this interview! I've been down in NOLA all week. I've hardly spent two hours in that house."

"I don't believe you," Sophie replied flatly. Truthfully, she didn't know what to think. He was the perfect suspect. The pair together explained everything. But his body language as she declared her disbelief came back as confusion more than the bitter resentment of a culprit caught out.

Kelly now shook from head to toe, his cell phone rattled against the table as he let out soft squeaks and half-words, his mind tumbling over how to prove where he'd been. Sophie felt an uneasy tension settle in her stomach. There was no way. If it wasn't him...

Sophie tilted her head. "Can you verify that?" she asked tentatively.

"I can," Greer said. He stood up. His expression was muted, professional. But as his eyes flitted from the skinny man to Sophie, she caught the slight tilt in his chin, the millimeter raise in his eyebrows. Doubt. "Mr. Kelly, may I have your car keys?"

Chapter 22

"I've thrown away our best lead." Sophie lay her head on the breakroom table at the Peillon police station. The cool plastic felt good on her forehead.

Greer set a fresh cup of coffee beside her, the machine still popping as the new brew settled in the carafe. "We ruled out a bad line. It happens."

He was trying to sound reassuring, but Sophie heard the resignation in his voice. He was disappointed too.

When Andrew Kelly handed over his keys, Greer was able to access the on-board computer for his Mini Cooper. The built-in GPS logged the vehicle's location, and a few minutes after the agent had plugged in his laptop, he showed Sophie the data.

Lines and lines of time stamps and coordinates. Andrew Kelly had been in New Orleans for a week, just as he said. Nowhere near Peillon until that morning when his GPS logged a request from the onboard screen for directions from a New Orleans hotel to Geoff Tamer's home address.

Ruling out Tamer's work van had been even simpler. The rusted wheel well and grime showed Greer that the tires hadn't been changed in month, perhaps years. And they did not match the tread marks from either crime scene.

"I pushed him too hard and he gave us a false memory," Sophie said, not for the first time since they reached the police station. "I don't even know if we're looking for a Mini Cooper at this point."

Greer sipped his coffee, settling into the chair beside Sophie with a soft groan. "Don't be too hard on yourself. You weren't lying earlier. Getting Cash to tell us what he saw was the best line we had. It still is, honestly."

The coffee cup smelled waxy, and the cream did little to conceal the acrid aroma, but as Greer shifted the cup a little closer, Sophie took it anyway.

"Look," Greer tapped his phone, 8:16 AM flashed up in illuminated letters. From Sophie's angle, they looked jumbled and backwards from the reflection in the cellphone's glass cover, and it took her a moment to translate the 91:8 that she saw. "We still have the better part of the day ahead of us. We can brainstorm, come up with a new angle, and maybe—"

Sophie abruptly sat up.

"A new angle," she murmured. Her eyes focused, her mind suddenly racing. "It's jumbled," she said in a breathy whisper, then again, more clearly. "It's jumbled!"

"What? What's jumbled?" Greer glanced at his phone, then back at Sophie.

With a shake of her head, she stood and started to pace the room. "I'm so stupid. Of course, I pushed Calloway and his brain tried to fill in the gaps. He saw the plate, but only vaguely, at a distance. He has the letters all jumbled in his head. Maybe only one of them is even right, but he saw them."

Greer slowly nodded, seeming to catch up with her line of thinking. "So we just look for other blue Mini Coopers."

"Forget the plate. It's wrong, it's not important. There can't be that many in the area." Sophie popped open her laptop, taking a quick pull of her coffee as it booted up.

Greer joined her, quickly adding. "I'll start with parishes west of the river. You start on the east side. Start close to the border and we'll work down towards New Orleans. Verify as you go if you can. They can't be far with all the planning they've had to do."

The pair set to work.

It wasn't long before the coffee was finished. They didn't take anymore, neither felt a lack of energy. They were onto something, Sophie could feel it, and with each name added she knew they were closer.

***

"Alright," Greer said at last, hanging up his cell phone and rubbing at his eyes. "That gives us—"

"Six," Sophie finished. "Six blue Mini Coopers registered within fifty miles. four really. Statistically, women are unlikely as killers. Particularly, in copycat cases." Sophie ticked a key on her laptop, like hammering a nail.

It wasn't until she'd said it that Sophie realized what she said. Copycat. Not RK. She wasn't ruling out the female suspects because she knew RK was male. She was ruling them out because they didn't fit the profile of a copycat killer or the methods of the killings. Her stomach twisted and she found herself biting back a tear. Clearing her throat to cover the expression, she tamped down the emotion bruiting through her nerves.

If Greer noticed, he didn't say anything, and Sophie silently thanked whatever providence had allowed it to happen. Discovering what manner of 'I told you so," Jonathan Greer preferred was not something she looked forward to finding out.

"We can set aside Mr. Tyson," Greer added. "His college verified he's been in New York for a series of guest lectures and won't be back for another week."

"Three, then," Sophie said.

"Two." Greer said. "Josiah Franklin, is simultaneously the owner of a blue Mini Cooper and interred at Greatmore Cemetery as of yesterday morning."

"Two."

"Two," Greer reiterated. For a moment the pair shared an eager grin. Each had one remaining suspect on their list. Sophie felt a thrill, her breath catching for a moment. They were so close. One of these two men had to be the killer.

It didn't take long for Greer's GPS tracker to lock down the vehicle's locations, but as Sophie reached his side of the table, Greer's grin vanished.

"Richard Knight," he read, "moving South-South East, about an hour away currently. The other—"

"Owen Bolton," Sophie read. "He's also headed south. That's the Jean Lafitte reserve."

Greer nodded, "Parked. No idea how long he's been there."

With a clap on the shoulder, Sophie slapped her laptop shut. "I'll take Bolton. See if you can get backup to cut off Knight while you catch up."

"No. We can both go after Knight. We know where Bolton is, local PD can—"

"Greer," Sophie said, quickly cutting him off. "We *don't* have time." Stepping to the breakroom door, Sophie held up her key fob. "We know what to look for. They don't."

Then, in a lower voice, moving away from her partner as he hurried to grab his own laptop, she said, "And not every killer waits for nightfall."

Chapter 23

It was a trap.

It had to be, because there was no way he could be this unlucky.

Wringing his hands along the faux-leather steering wheel, Greer knew that wasn't true. Bad luck had seasoned his life so often that he could only faintly recognize the flavor of it. He simply hadn't expected it to be so... challenging?

Sweeping around a sluggish minivan with a single click of his turn signal and a rumble from the spurred engine, he thought about that word. Challenging. Was that really the word for Sophie Quinn? It was certainly the most diplomatic term that leapt to mind. Other contenders like 'spooky' and 'unpredictable' didn't seem to quite capture the feeling. 'Unlucky'? That was a no-brainer. And 'trap'... well, he couldn't put that on her. Not really.

Deputy Director Hitchens had made his dissatisfaction with Greer and Special Agent Merchant apparent. Internal investigations seldom made friends, but Greer's unwillingness to stay silent had earned the Director's ire as surely as Merchant had by shielding him from reprisal.

So it hadn't taken much creative thinking to put the pieces together when Hitchens OK'd Merchant's request to bring in Quinn and immediately paired her with him.

Three birds, one stone.

One screw up, and Hitchens could get his wish. All three of them gone.

But the truly frustrating part was that it was working.

Greer shook his head. He'd picked a lock on a suspect's trailer, disabled a police station camera, and raided an ex-con's home on evidence that didn't officially exist, obtained by hypnosis. Why? What was wrong with him?

Greer's gaze flicked from the GPS display on his cell phone to the cracked asphalt of Highway 10 as it tore by under him, breaking around the sparse traffic like a NASCAR driver gunning for the checkered flag. Richard Knight's Mini Cooper was still on the highway, and backup was en route to assist in the stop, but the response to his call for support seemed sluggish and uncoordinated. He'd been on the line with them three times already trying to wrangle a net around their, hopefully, unsuspecting target. He wondered if Quinn had even bothered calling for backup. The woman's drive and self-sufficiency was maddening for someone like him, drilled in military teamwork and the strength of the group.

Then again, Greer didn't think Sophie was in this for the greater good. To her it was personal. He could see it in the way she attacked each new lead. She wasn't a woman who weathered storms. She was the storm, and anything that got in her way would be sure to feel it. Another time he would have admired that about her. The will to look monsters in the eye wasn't something to scoff about... but you couldn't fight every monster. Greer knew where that road led. When you try to slay every dragon, you become the dragon. You lose everything.

A text bubble blossomed on the phone's screen.

U drive a hard bargain.

Greer blinked then gave a short laugh, shaking his head as the grim thoughts that loomed over him slipped away, brushed aside like crumbs from a table. He didn't need to open the message in full, she'd be too busy with her own work to talk anyway.

The small picture of his daughter, Kinsley, appeared beside the message, her broad smile and cherry red curls filling out the tiny bubble like an antique cameo. It was hard to believe she was going into her senior year of high school. One more summer as a camp counselor at *Camp New Trails*. Maybe she'd go back to it between semesters at college? She hadn't said... or maybe she had, Greer suddenly couldn't remember. He would ask when they talked next. Hopefully tonight or the day after. When the planets aligned and they actually got to see each other in person...

He tapped the message to dismiss it, the full chain appearing for a brief second as his forefinger brushed the screen.

This is so crazy! I can't believe ur working with THE Sophie Quinn.

can you get an autograph?

I have that t-shirt from her NY special. Kaleidoscope.

Please??? I'll do dishes and *laundry this week.*

2 weeks?

2 weeks and dishes for the rest of the month?!

>: (

U drive a hard bargain.

Briefly brainstorming the least awkward way to ask Miss Quinn for her autograph, Greer didn't see the flashing lights behind him until the police siren wound up.

"Pull over!" the cop added from the car-mounted speaker.

Greer threw up a palm, anger curdling in his chest. They did not have time for this.

Snatching the phone, he called back the station.

"What's going on?" Greer snapped. "I'm getting flagged on 10."

"Negative, Agent Greer. We're pulling over the suspect now. A white Taurus sedan—"

Greer tapped the side of the phone against his forehead, giving himself a few soft knocks as he took a steadying breath. "*I'm* the white sedan," he growled into the phone. "Powder blue, Mini Cooper. I clock it at—" Greer swiped the screen of his phone, switching back to the GPS for a moment, "Three miles ahead."

The dispatcher's side grumbled distantly in the way speakers do when someone shoves their hand over the microphone.

"Roger that, Agent Greer," they responded sheepishly, the word cut off as Greer hung up.

With a wave through the driver's window, the police car pulled forward, coming alongside Greer. They exchanged a few swift hand signals and Greer gave the officer a nod as he tapped the brake, letting the police cruiser pull ahead.

With sirens running, the police escort cut through the highway traffic. Greer no longer had to adjust course as they blew past line after line of cars. Mile markers ticked by like street signs in the suburbs.

When they finally caught sight of the Mini Cooper, the escort pulled over, using the lights and siren to guide the driver onto the shoulder. Greer pulled ahead, parking in front to stop any potential getaway.

He steeled himself. Every highway murderer he could think of flashing through his mind. Thoughts of severed limbs in trunks and victims folded into suitcases. Roadside killers often brought their prey to a second location for a kill. But Knight had pulled over right away. He wasn't afraid to be stopped.

And that made Greer nervous.

"Richard Knight," Greer said, joining the officer by the Cooper's driver side door.

The man's initial look of annoyance was replaced by concern at the tan-suited FBI Agent's approach. A bushy beard under sharp cheek-bones, jostled with half-formed questions as the suspect hung his wrists loosely over the wheel.

"That's me," he answered. "What's this—"

Greer's hand rested ready by his pistol grip and the other jerked the car door open.

"Step out of the car." His tone brooked no negotiation and as the man stumbled out, led back by the assisting officer, Greer set to searching the car.

"Hey! What are you doing?" Knight called out, his beard whipping with highway wind. "You can't just pull me over for no reason, man!"

It was not a large car. There were not a lot of places to hide tools or victims as Greer swept his hand under the seats and popped the meager trunk.

"There's nothing in there. You got no right!" Knight was shuffling now, his feet scuffing the pavement as his shoulders turned in a nearly motionless form of pacing, the assisting officer ready to grab him if he made a move.

Greer slipped a hand under the trunk's floor mat. He brushed something. It crinkled under his fingers as he pinched it.

Knight's face went pale, his mouth flapping while his brain frantically tried to find the words.

Then, as Greer held up a palm-sized packet, Knight shouted, "You planted that! I've never seen that in my life. You can't prove it's mine."

Greer's mouth drew into a hard line.

A fifty-fifty shot. And he'd missed.

Damn it! I should have stayed with her. I knew splitting up was a bad idea.

But it was too late to reconsider. Too late to change course. Quinn was miles away with no way to reach her before she caught up with the killer.

He tossed the bag back into the trunk as he thrust his phone up to his ear. "Miss Quinn. Knight's a bust. Nothing but a dime-bag of weed. Wait for backup." He took a deep breath, his stomach clenching as he hustled back to his sedan. "Dammit, pick up! It's Bolton! The killer is Bolton!"

Chapter 24

Coral snakes.

As Sophie raced along the wooden walkways and high-ground trails of the Jean Lafitte National Historical Park and Reserve, she again found it odd, the places the mind will go when death is on the line.

A coral snake, and she had no doubt there were many of them hiding in the waterways and bayou marsh surrounding her, can deliver up to twenty milligrams of venom in a single bite. She'd read that once when she was nine years old. Page thirty-two of the *Field Guide to the Gulf Coast*. Her photographic memory even brought her the red, black, and yellow banding of the scales shown in the accompanying picture.

She had also read on that same page that as little as four milligrams were sufficient to kill an adult man. That meant a single bite from a coral snake held enough potency to drop five people dead.

Owen Bolton had killed three so far.

She didn't know what that meant, or if it meant anything at all. But as she passed a pair of hikers powerwalking where alligators, cottonmouths, and coral snakes called home, she warned them the way she would for any dangerous animal.

"Excuse me. FBI. We're evacuating the park. We believe there is a dangerous person on the grounds. Please leave right away."

The hikers gave her the same startled look and hurried nod that the old man reading by a lakeside had—and the mother pushing a stroller along the broad path nearest the parking lot.

The morning mist had settled. Hanging cypress and moss-covered gum trees waded like fishermen through the slow-moving waters and collected the dew like sweat on their knotted, wooden tendons. The smell of algae and dark, sucking earth mingled with the wet-leaf scent of the previous night's rain.

Was that someone by the lakeside? Sophie leaned over the boardwalk's edge, squinting around the shady trees. She slapped the wooden railing, turning to hustle to the lakeside where she could get a better look.

She had to hurry.

The Mini Cooper had stood out in the parking lot beside the visitor's center. No one was in the car, but it matched Owen Bolton's plate. Cut zip ties lay on the floor of the passenger seat and a black satchel was visible in the trunk. A clear bottle poked out of it with an obscured label that Sophie instantly recognized.

Chloroform. Just like she had smelled in the first two victims' hotel room at the Cotton House.

Park security had seemed to take Sophie's warning to heart. Concerned faces and hurried phone calls as the two wide-eyed young men immediately started calling in more security officers as well as the police. They broke out a map, showing Sophie the park and stammering out a plan to help the police when they got there.

But it would take time. Time that the victim didn't have.

Sophie checked her phone. The deeper she entered the preserve, the worse her signal became. She saw she had a missed call from Greer, but she hadn't felt or heard the ringing. No message yet.

She stowed her phone again.

No sign of anyone by the lake now. Sophie jogged further along. An alligator lazed across the path, its tail sticking out of the tall grass by the edge of the walkway. Sophie leaned down as she passed, giving the tail a quick tap that sent the gator skittering forward, back into the murky water with a splash.

No one likes being snuck up on, no matter how many teeth they have.

What are you planning? Sophie thought desperately, slowing down, trying not to miss any errant clearings or hidden pockets where a killer might hurriedly take an unwilling victim. They had to be alive still. He couldn't just carry a dead body into the park for disposal, not in the middle of the day.

He also wouldn't use zip ties if he was transporting a corpse. No, there was some ritual here. Some event or method he was trying to duplicate.

Sophie chewed her lip, closing her eyes for a moment as she paused in the path. The names from Andrew Kelly's true crime blog scrolled past in a blur. Parks. Swamps. Water. Alligators. Zip Ties, chloroform, morning—

"Dates." Sophie held up a hand, tracing her finger through the air as she turned back through her memories for the details.

"Norman Gummer," she said quietly. The Bayou Bluebeard. He would charm women, invite them out on dates with him in the park, out to secluded lakesides and ponds. But this killer had taken this victim by force...

Of course he had.

The ideas were falling together quickly now. Sophie's eyes moved behind her closed lids like REM sleep. The killer was a copycat, trying to emulate the murderers he read about. But he couldn't do it. He changes the script to cover his shortcomings.

He chained his victims to the bayou trees because he's not RK and was afraid they wouldn't be found.

He hired Cash Calloway to kidnap Elijah because he's not the Memphis Butcher and couldn't figure out how to take the young man himself.

And he chloroformed a young woman, dragging her out to the bayou to kill her, because he's not Norman Gummer. He's not charming and a part of him knows it—knows that he's a fraud.

It fits. And that means...

"He's going to drown her."

Sophie turned sharply. She knew where she needed to be. Her mind broke down the park map she'd glanced at with park security and isolated a pocket of small lakes, just off the main trails.

That's where he'd be. Out of the way, near water. Somewhere in that tangle of ponds and creeks.

But would she be looking for a hostage, or a body?

Chapter 25

The kill had to be perfect.

This side trail was part of the preserve, and unlike the boardwalks and dry dirt paths around the sunlit park, the narrow trail slipped between trees like a shy man hurrying through a busy street.

Three small ponds, tied together by the lazy currents of bayou creeks. She would check each one. The killer would have to bring the victim to the edge of the water. Norman Gummer's MO demanded that the victim be walked out into the shallows at knifepoint. He wouldn't change that part. The *actual* kill would have to be perfect in his mind. Everything before and after was mutable, but the kill itself had to ring true.

If it didn't, Sophie's degree in criminology told her what would happen. He'd grow even more unstable. Erratic. His carefully calculated murders could become a rampage, taking as many people as he could then likely taking his own life.

Sophie caught the glint of sun on water and broke from the trail, crashing through rushes and tall grass. The pond spread out in front of her, a hundred feet on a side with a squashed curve to it like a jellybean.

A flash of movement to her right drew Sophie's eye, and she nearly reached for her gun. It was a man in a khaki vest holding a pair of binoculars in one hand, a journal and a mechanical pencil gripped together in the other. He gave her a puzzled look, probably wondering what a woman in a professional suit coat and office slacks was doing ankle-deep in marsh mud.

Sophie looked into the water beside him. No young woman floating in the muck.

Alone. His expression more curious than concerned. Dressed for birdwatching, not a Sunday date.

Not the killer.

Sophie returned his awkward wave with a flash of her ID. "FBI. Clear the park."

She didn't waste time seeing if the man would comply. Instead, she continued along the pond's edge. She could see where the flow fed from the next connected body of water further ahead.

She nearly stepped on a pair of young lovers tangled in the shade of a gum tree. Skeptical at first, she quickly ruled out the young man. Judging by her enthusiastic pawing, his date seemed to want to be there; not the behavior of a woman zip-tied and chloroformed within the last few hours.

"Pack it up," Sophie ordered, clearing her throat when the couple didn't immediately respond. The young man shouted some profanity or another, but Sophie firmly locked her expression in stone-faced judgment, and the college-aged boy quickly wilted under her stare, fetching his date's shirt from the swamp grass.

Sophie had worked for years in entertainment and a bit of skin was not going to make her blush. Costume switches with only a curtain between herself and the audience and shared changing rooms in her early days of group performances had done a lot to remove the mystique of the human body.

Not that she was immune to the charms of a fit, athletic form. One of the first signs that she'd really made it as a performer came in the unending string of young men with bleached teeth and rock-hard abs asking if she'd 'hypnotize them'. It was flattering at first, then annoying, and finally infuriating. She was a world-class performer, with an eidetic memory, breaking new ground in hypnotism and mentalism. But to them, she was simply a sugar momma, a hot twenty-something with a mansion in Cali, they could stay with if she would let them.

Sophie traveled so much for her work, she was barely in her own home, and it had taken less than a month for the empty-headed himbos to lose all their charm.

The second pond was the same as the first. No bodies floating in the slow waters, a few stragglers on nature hikes. Sophie's heart was pounding. If he wasn't here, she'd lose even more time backtracking. But this was the only option that made sense. Wasn't it?

The second pond's edge curled, funneling towards the creek connecting the final bit of the bayou's constellation.

Then a shape caught her eye. On the pond's far side, staring over the water in the direction of the morning sun. Two figures.

A man and a woman.

She was in a skirt patterned with sunflowers, the yellow buds exaggerating the blond of her hair, hanging loose over her shoulders. He wore a loose polo and nice slacks of similarly bright material, a couple's outfit. His dark hair was slicked back, and his clean-shaven face let the sunlight contrast every crack in his wide smile. He leaned beside her with one arm behind her back, the other crossing over his own waist and holding her by the hand. Everything in his stance spoke of ease, control. He was whispering something in the woman's ear.

For a brief moment, Sophie thought it may be another couple enjoying the preserve. Then she froze, her eyes locked as she took in the scene.

The woman's posture was stiff. Her shoulders bunched. Defensive. Her feet angled away from the man, her hand hung loose in his, held there by force. Her hips unnaturally still, indicating a tightness in her spine.

He has a knife at her back, maybe a gun, Sophie thought.

Now she saw in the man's older face, a wide-eyed enthusiasm. An excitement that only exaggerated the watery-eyed fear and trembling lips of his companion. No, his hostage.

There was a bridge ahead, she could round the lake at the creek crossing. But the man was looking across the open water, the reflection of the sun shining up into his eyes and forcing him to look towards the crossing. If she came that way, she'd be seen.

She had to find another way to him.

Sophie looked at the murky water ahead of her. If she crossed where the water was deeper, the morning sun would help shield her. She'd be moving in his blind spot. If she came out of the water on that side, she may even have a clean shot at him. Sophie scanned the water, squinting to scrutinize the floating branches and dark reeds. She'd seen one gator today already, and she thought of the coral snakes again.

Another person may have hesitated, turned back and gone for help or accepted that the killer would see them approach and stick to high ground. But she grew up around water like this, and she'd been dealing with *snakes* since she was a child.

Sophie looked down at her cell phone, suppressing a grimace. It didn't have a signal anyway. She folded her suit coat and set the phone down beside the nearest tree.

Crouching, she shuffled through the grass, taking no chances. She drew her pistol and held it beside her cheek, keeping it above the waterline to keep it dry. A wet gun wasn't guaranteed to misfire, but this wasn't the time to take unnecessary risks.

The cool water rose over her ankles, then her knees. Hunched, making the most use of the concealing murk, she walked until the water covered her to the shoulder. She felt the shifting of fish around her hips and the rustle of silt at her feet.

A fat catfish the size of a Doberman gave her a wide-mouthed glare and smacked her with a flapping tail as it swam away. Sophie froze. The killer was now close enough that he would hear splashes like that.

If he did, he ignored it. Instead, he gently pushed the girl in front of him, stepping behind her like a nagging thought. Thirty feet to Sophie's right, the girl entered the water, stepping to her ankles, then her knees.

Sophie felt the ground rising again, another twenty feet to the shore if she kept the distance between her and the killer. Ten feet.

The blond woman was in water up to her waist now, her sunflower skirt swirling among the sparse reeds.

Sophie saw the knife in the killer's hand as he put a guiding hand on the woman's shoulder, pushing her down from behind, making her kneel, the water now between her chin and lips as tears flowed down her face.

No time now.

Sophie rose from the water like a snapping gator, a geyser shooting up around her shoulders as she leveled the gun at the knife-wielding man.

"Freeze! FBI! Drop the knife!"

The woman in the water gasped, the man beside her looking similarly shocked and nearly fumbling the three-inch pocketknife he'd had at her back.

Sophie stepped forward, giving him no time for consideration. Soaked to her neck and knee-deep in the water herself, she was only twenty feet away, moving between the killer and the shoreline. He wouldn't be able to run in water that deep. She had a gun, and he had a knife.

The briefest moment of consideration flitted behind the man's eyes. Then his jaw set, his brow furrowed.

And Sophie knew instantly, there would be no surrender.

Her pistol barked as Sophie took a shot, aiming high and wide of the woman kneeling in the water, trying to catch the killer's chest while she still had a clear target. At that same moment, the man spun, folding over the crying woman like a cape, and the bullet broke the water behind them with a sharp splash.

His empty hand grabbed his hostage's hair, jerking her up as he swiftly sidled behind her. His knife flew to her throat, and the woman screamed.

Sophie had no clear shot now. Owen Bolton, the copycat killer, held his final victim as a human shield between him and the gun, one hand in her golden hair, the other pressing a serrated pocketknife to her neck.

Chapter 26

Sophie didn't tell Bolton that the game was up. She didn't say to surrender or try to bluff that she had a whole SWAT team closing in on them.

People who think they have no escape fight to the death. People who think they have no options will kill the hostage and then themselves. He had been so careful, so diligent and methodical. Now, he was furious. Sophie could see that in his tense, white-knuckle grip. But he wasn't ready to lose it all. His eyes flicked to the shoreline behind Sophie. He shifted his footing, trying not to sink in the bayou's muck.

He was thinking.

"Help me! Please!" the woman in his grip screamed. Her words were raw, cracking with sobs as she shuddered with fear.

"It's going to be Ok," Sophie said, quietly, calmly. She didn't look away from Bolton. Her gun and attention were entirely focused on his body language, the angry scrutiny his dark eyes gave her and the swamp around them.

He's wondering what Norman Gummer would do, Sophie thought. Or maybe Hoffrey Timms, or RK, or any of the dozen other killers he no doubt worshipped. Maybe that was her road in.

"I've been following your work," Sophie said. She let the words sink in for a breath. "The River Killer. The Memphis Butcher. Now the Bayou Bluebeard." She leaned into the names the media had given them. Their legend would be what attracted him to them, why he copied them.

Bolton's lips curled. Suspicion.

"Then you know that I'll kill her if you take e'en one step closer," he answered.

Sophie nodded. "I believe you. I haven't, and I won't." It was true. Since their standoff started, Sophie had only sidled parallel with the shore, but she'd not come any closer. A fight in the deeper water would only favor the man with the knife. "Honestly, it's impressive," she continued. "I double-checked to be sure Timms hadn't escaped from prison. It was... striking, how exact your display was."

Bolton smirked. Sophie could see the wheels turning in his mind. Taking in the compliment, immediately caching it as a trick by the naïve FBI agent to get him to lower his guard. His smile broadened, ticking slightly as he tried to suppress the expression.

Duper's Delight.

Pulling the knife away, he waved the blade around in a cavalier gesture. "You talk about it like you know the cases. You're FBI, right? Probably some BAU shrink they pulled after the local boys lost their lunch. Am I warm?"

Sophie blinked, stiffening a little. Letting her body language read 'shocked'. She nodded hesitantly. "That's right."

"Then you and I both know how this goes? If you don't let me walk away, I cut her throat." The woman in the sundress flinched, a choked cry silenced by the sudden pressure of the knife warning her against an outburst. "I'll die," Bolton continued. "Likely by that gun in your hands, but she'll still be dead." He paused, Sophie guessed with the intention of letting her imagine the hostage lying dead in the swamp around them.

Sophie bit her lip. Tension coiled in her stomach that she didn't need to affect. Her options for getting his victim out alive were not great and Bolton knew it. But he thought he was in control, and that could be an advantage all on its own. He had laid out the likely course, quickly and confidently.

He's getting it off the table, Sophie thought. *He wants me to make a deal with him.*

Trepidation drove her heart faster as Sophie tried to sort through the hundreds of hours she'd spent studying killers for her PhD. Serial killers were usually not fond of deals. After they were caught and imprisoned perhaps, but not while they were holding a victim hostage. Not with a knife in their hands.

He's not finished, Sophie realized. This isn't just about copying killers. He has a larger plan. His own method? A way to make his mark? So what was this... practice? Prelude?

He wants to be unique...

Sophie pulled back the pistol. Bolton watched her, his eyes as focused as a coyote as she turned the barrel to the side... and ejected the clip.

Holding up the pistol's magazine, she let Bolton see it, let him see the line of loaded bullets. Then she tossed it into the saw grass behind her.

"Take me instead," Sophie said, holstering her now empty pistol. "Let her go."

The murderer's face screwed up, his lips curling in a suspicious sneer. "What kind of trick is this?" Bolton snapped.

"No trick," Sophie replied. "You're right. Someone is ending up dead. But I swore an oath..." Sophie pointed to the ground, her chin raised, the defiance of a martyr in her voice, captivating him, lulling him with the subtle movements of her eyes and hands. "I swore to protect innocent lives. Let her go. I'm unarmed and not going anywhere."

It didn't matter that she wasn't technically an FBI agent, that she had in fact taken no oaths, or that she'd already shot at him once. He'd already let her know what he thought she was... she only had to go along with the idea.

Bolton eyed the folded grass where the clip had landed. He was shuffling closer now, water running off him and his hostage as they entered the shallows. Sophie backed off to accommodate the motion, drawing him closer to the shore. As her heel hit firm ground, the killer and hostage now stood in ankle-deep muck.

"You wanted this. I can tell, it's been part of your plan all along," Sophie said to the killer. "To do something no one else has done before. To prove you're better than the investigators that caught Gummer—and Timms—all of them."

Stepping on the shore, Bolton was only loosely holding the knife, his hand clenching his victim's hair relaxed.

He was listening to her story, she could see him visualizing what it would be like. What the papers and blogs would say. *Masquerade Killer Slays Investigator, FBI Stunned.* She teased the fantasy, drawing out her words.

"I came here on a hunch," Sophie said. "No one else believed me. Kill me instead. You get a chance to continue your work with all the notoriety of a dead FBI agent behind you."

Bolton licked his lips. He was only six feet away. Now four. The knife shifted as he tightened his grip. He kept his eyes on Sophie, weighing her words.

At least, that was what he wanted her to believe.

His feet were set, his hips squared and his legs tensed.

The murderer's mind was made up.

With a shove, Owen Bolton threw aside his hostage, sending her reeling into the damp tall-grass. His knife hand shot forward, a venomous sneer on his lips as the steel fang lashed out for Sophie's throat.

Fingers trained on sleight of hand slipped to her holster as quick as running water. Sophie snatched up the pistol, firing it in one smooth motion.

She'd ejected the clip... but that left one shot still in the chamber.

Bolton screamed, his leg shuddering as the bullet buried in his thigh. Sophie threw her free arm up, catching Bolton's attack and stopping the knife over her shoulder. Tumbling into her, the killer's free hand grabbed Sophie's collar for stability, and the pair fell into the sawgrass, Bolton on top of her, damp earth staining them both as fingers clawed for wrists, and knees and ankles wrestled for control of the melee.

Hot breath on her neck, Sophie felt the serrated edge of the pocketknife's three-inch blade as it ripped at her shirt above her left shoulder. She had dropped her pistol and now held the knife at bay with one forearm and a hand gripped over her attacker's wrist.

Bolton let out a feral growl, trying to climb higher, to push his heavier body over the knife and drive it into Sophie's throat. As he did, he splayed his legs for stability, and Sophie drove her knee into his groin.

With a wincing gasp, Bolton's arms shuddered, weakening as his body instinctively curled to protect his battered manhood. As his head dropped, Sophie drove her own forehead forward in a headbutt. Cartilage crunched and the front of her close-cut hair came away wet.

“My nose! You broke my damn nose!”

Rolling to the side, Bolton’s free hand flew to his face, blood running between his fingers as he let out a hacking gasp. He was laying on his back now, the knife swiping blindly as Sophie crawled to her knees, pulling out of reach.

Suddenly one rage-filled eye locked onto her, and a flailing foot shot out in a mule kick straight for Sophie’s chest. Her sternum creaked and Sophie felt her vision flash white as she fell against the rope-like roots of a nearby cypress.

“Try to trick me! I’ll kill you! You think you can save her? You won’t.” Bolton let out a cry of pain as he tried to regain his feet, his gun-shot leg collapsing under him.

Sophie couldn’t breathe. The wind knocked out of her, she let out a gurgling gasp, but her lungs wouldn’t fill. She fumbled for the tree, trying to drag herself to her feet as her heels slipped in the wet ground. Bolton spat blood, his hand coming away from his bent nose as he moved to Sophie’s side on hands and knees like a stalking tarantula.

The knife flashed forward and Sophie felt a sting at her hip. A flash of pain that she didn’t have the oxygen to scream for.

“I’ll kill you!” Bolton raved. “Then I’ll find her and kill her too. I’ll kill a hundred more, you stupid bitch!”

The knife shot forward again. This time, it went straight for Sophie’s heart.

Pain. Stinging pain.

But not in her chest. Her back against the cypress, Bolton reaching over her prone legs, both of Sophie's arms had come forward. Her mouth drew into a hard line while blood ran between her fingers.

She had grabbed the knife by the blade.

Sophie gripped the small blade in one hand, her other holding Bolton's wrist.

Pressing her thumb into the tendons, Bolton screamed and his fingers loosened. Sophie jerked the blade out of his hand by the edge, and in one swift swipe, slammed the blunt, metal handle of the pocketknife directly against the murderer's temple.

Bolton went limp, his heavy body falling over her legs like a sleeping child.

Breathing heavily, her lungs stinging as they remembered how to breathe, Sophie closed the knife.

"Is he dead?" The woman in the sunflower skirt tip-toed closer.

Sophie wasn't sure. And she pressed a finger to his throat.

She blinked, her eyebrows beetling in confusion. Two beats. She felt two pulses. The momentary confusion passed as she realized her leg felt hot. And wet.

Sophie rolled the killer off of her, examining the red stain seeping from the stab wound in her hip.

"Huh," she murmured. "That's... that's a lot of blood."

Chapter 27

"That *is* a lot of blood," Greer commented, giving an approving whistle while also somehow managing to look embarrassed.

"Right?" Sophie shifted the hospital bedsheet to cover the red bandages, only realizing afterward that her forty-year-old partner may not be used to seeing so much skin on women he had just met, and his inquiry on her wound may not have been an invitation for her to show off the stitching.

Sophie decided to take pity on the man and gestured to a pitcher of water resting on the far side of the room, letting him take a moment to fill a water cup for her and gather himself. She used her bandaged hand to really sell the pity angle on the gesture, thankful that the cut had been shallow and there was no muscle or nerve damage.

"Did Merchant tell you about the journal?" Greer asked as he handed over the cool drink.

"No. A manifesto?" she answered curiously.

"Not quite. It's a lot of clipping and sporadic notes. He's been planning this for almost a year. Obsessively." Greer's eyebrows flared in emphasis as he shook his head at the memory. "He had been following dozens of people, mainly around Peillon. Names, details, routines. We have local PD checking up on them right now. Making sure everyone's safe."

"God..."

"So far everyone is," Greer continued. "The early pages have details about four or five serial killers. The ones you surmised already. RK. Timms—"

"Norman Gummer?" she asked.

Greer pointed to her in affirmation. "Him too. Those were his choices. His... I don't know, *muses* I guess. But the later pages are just plans. Ideas. It looks like he was coming up with his own method, combining ideas from other serial killers."

Sophie's stomach tightened. She had been right. He had been gearing up for something bigger. They had come so close. "Another hour and he would have gotten another... but I still don't understand why."

Greer clicked his tongue. "The gang in the Behavioral Analysis Unit will have a field day parsing that out. But the way he writes about these killers in his journal... It's like a kid trying to impress his parents. Like he's asking them if he's good enough." Greer took a seat, rolling his elbow over the back of the chair as settled back. "I did a little digging while you were still out. Turns out that Owen Bolton is adopted.

He put in a request for information on his birth parents a couple years back, and it looks like that lines up with the week his adoptive mother passed. I'm thinking it may have been one of those deathbed confessions or something like that. That maybe he didn't know he was adopted."

Sophie chewed her lip, considering the new information. "But why would that set him off?"

Raising a finger, Greer said. "I think that might have more to do with what he found out about his birth mother. I had Merchant help me with that. No information on the father, but he went up for adoption after his mother was murdered. The kid was less than a year old. Still unsolved it seems, her murder, I mean."

Sophie let out a long sigh. "His whole life fell apart and the only living connection he had was to an unknown murderer."

Her stomach knotted, and Sophie clenched the edge of her bedsheets. She thought about her own life, broken, distant from her parents... her sister Molly long dead. The smoky voice. Inviting and cold, like a mausoleum door.

Jus' like you and me, eh, cher? Two peas in a pod. Living happily. Ever. After.

"Miss Quinn?"

Sophie opened her eyes. Greer was standing, looking at her nervously. "Are you alright? Do you need a nurse?"

She shook her head hurriedly. "Sorry," she answered, waving off his concern. "Just a stitch in my side. I'm fine."

A knock at the door. Sophie shifted on her elbow and Greer stood up, his arms going behind his back like a soldier at attention. Her honey-brown eyes dancing briefly between the two of them, the lithe Lidya Merchant stepped through the hospital door.

"Quinn. You look well."

Sophie laughed, a short yip that disappeared into a wince at the pain prodding her hip bone.

"Thank you, ma'am," she managed, receiving a quick nod from the severe, older woman in response.

"I have to say, well done. To both of you," Merchant added, giving a separate tip of her head to Greer. "Fast and effective. And it doesn't hurt that I get to personally rub this success in Hitchens' face back at the office."

The only indication that her comment had been a joke was the slight tug at the corner of her mouth, but Sophie grinned along all the same. "Glad to oblige."

"Still," Merchant stepped closer, her voice lowering by a degree. "It would probably behoove you to keep your reports *simple.* No need to invite further inquiry, right?"

Something in that look told Sophie that her and Greer's tactics hadn't been entirely unnoticed, but then again, Lidya Merchant had a tendency to make everyone who looked into her light brown eyes feel undressed. She may simply be guessing that the two of them couldn't help but make trouble.

Greer gave a clipped, "Understood," as Sophie nodded in agreement.

Then, like a grandmother finished scolding and ready to dote on her grandchildren once again, her expression softened. She leaned forward as she said to Sophie, "Detroit will be happy to have you back... though, I have to say, we'll miss you down here. Solid work, Quinn."

Without waiting for a reply, Merchant stood, slipping her sunglasses over her face and turning for the door. "We've set you up at the hotel across from the field office. You can stay a few more days while you rest up, then we'll get your flight arranged and ship you back on home."

Home.

Sophie lay back. Thinking about her parent's pink trailer, the children playing in the creeks; the crawdad boil and sizzling catfish, her heart heavy.

Because it wasn't real, and it wasn't hers. Her home was Detroit.

And she had to go back.

Epilogue

"You have one more chance. One. Then I'm burying you in the swamp."

Sophie jerked the blue blouse out of the open suitcase laying on her hotel bed. Untangling the collar button from the lacy fringe hanging off the sleeve, she grabbed the shoulders and attempted a fresh fold, only for the lace to grab the zipper of her jeans, pulling the fabric out of her hands as she lifted it.

A moment later, the trash bin beside the hotel dresser bumbled against the wall, the impact of the thrown shirt having sent it teetering.

It wasn't really the blouse's fault, Sophie acknowledged with a quick breath. She had been on edge for two days now. The pain from the stab wound and the shallow slice in her hand was manageable but made sleeping difficult. She woke up every time she rolled in her sleep, with a shooting pain through her hip bone.

But that wasn't really what was keeping her awake.

She had really thought it would be him. When Meyer had handed her the file and sent her out from Detroit, her blood had burned. Now... now, she only felt cold.

How many years would it be before the River Killer surfaced again? How long would she have to wait, her ear to the ground, her eyes straining for any sign of him?

Maybe Greer was right... she had made this case about finding her personal boogeyman. It had taken him standing his ground with her and a mountain of evidence before she opened up to other possibilities.

But what if he never appeared? Serial killers didn't just stop. They kept doing what they did until they were caught or they were dead. And that... that terrified her more than any flashback. What if the reason RK never resurfaced was because he was already dead?

A knock at the door roused Sophie from her ruminations. She checked the time on her cellphone. Her ride shouldn't be here for another hour.

Stepping to the door, Sophie looked through the peep hole.

A lanky man with skin that looked deep-fried from the sun's kisses stood on the other side. He had a well-waxed mustache, turned up at the corners of his mouth and wore a straw trilby over black hair pulled into a ponytail the same color as his loose, flowing shirt.

"Miss Sophie, I do not mind waiting, but, *eh*, given as we both know you're in there, can we speak, face to face, as it were?"

Sophie pulled the chain on the door and opened it, stepping aside to let the lean man in.

"Fabian," she said curiously. "I wasn't expecting you. Come in."

"*Merci*," Fabian St. Claire said, stepping inside, the Texas in his voice giving an oddly bold color to the Creole expression. "I won't take too much of your time, Miss Sophie. We just have some business, and I understand you're planning to fly the coop right soon."

Sophie folded her arms, leaning back against the dresser. "You keeping tabs on me now, Fabian?"

The man's face stretched in animated embarrassment, "No, no, no, nothing like that. I only mean that with that copycat killer cinched up, you're likely headed back to Detroit, amiright?" His teeth clacked as Fabian pressed a cough drop to the corner of his mouth, his shoulders hunching while he broke Dee-troit into two discrete words.

"I don't understand," Sophie cut in. "Did my payment not go through? I didn't need anything but that information on the Lamberts. Thank you for that, by the by."

"No trouble at all, Miss Sophie. But no, your payment came through just fine. This isn't about the Lamberts or that copycat, Owen Bolton."

"What is this about then?" Sophie prompted.

Meeting her eye, Fabian tilted his head sympathetically. His voice lowering to nearly a whisper. "It's about the River Killer."

Sophie's breath caught. Fabian didn't wait for a reply though. He leaned back against the hotel wall, his hands finding the pockets of his slacks. "You've always been a good client, Miss Sophie. Pay on time. Enthusiastic. I like to keep my eyes out for good clients, you know?"

Sophie's mind was spinning. There had been nothing, for years only whispers and hints, dead ends and total fabrications. But Fabian never lied. Never exaggerated. Everything he'd given her was solid, even when it led to a dead end, it didn't lead there by his own negligence.

"What did you find?" she asked, her throat suddenly dry.

"Murders," Fabian flapped his elbows with a subtle shrug. "His murders. Maybe his *first* murders. Not the nine we know about. Earlier... messier." Stepping forward, Fabian clacked his cough drop and tipped up his hat, scratching at his scalp with his ring finger. "I would love to give this information to you. If you want to renew our contract. Same price as before, just where we left off? Maybe I see what else I can find."

Sophie's throat caught. If she was being honest with herself, she didn't have that kind of money anymore. Not for long anyway. But did it matter? If she caught him... if she put RK down once and for all, she could go back. TV specials. Live shows in Vegas. She'd make the money back. If this was what Fabian said it was, she didn't need to last six more years... just long enough to catch the man who destroyed her family.

"Deal."

Sophie extended a handshake.

Fabian St. Claire smiled and slapped his hand into hers. "Ha! Ça c'est bon, Miss Sophie."

When he pulled his fingers free, a USB drive appeared in Sophie's palm. Squat and metallic, the cap attached by a black plastic hinge.

The thin, excitable man tipped his straw hat, stepping to the doorway. "I'll show myself out. It looks like you have some studying to do."

Setting down the USB, Sophie agreed. But first, she had a flight to cancel.

Also by Georgia Wagner

Ella Porter Series

Once a rising star in the FBI, with the best case closure rate of any investigator, Ella Porter is now exiled to a small gold mining town bordering the wilderness of Alaska. The reason for her new assignment? She allowed a prolific serial killer to escape custody.

But what no one knows is that she did it on purpose.

THE RIVER'S SECRET

The day she shows up in Nome, bags still unpacked, the wife of the richest gold miner in town goes missing. This is the second woman to vanish in as many days. And it's up to Ella to find out what happened.

Assigning Ella to Nome is no accident, either. Though she swore she'd never return, Ella grew up in the small, gold mining town, treated like royalty as a child due to her own family's wealth. But like all gold tycoons, the Porter family secrets are as dark as Ella's own.

Also by Georgia Wagner

Artemis Blythe Mystery

The skeletons in her closet are twitching...

Genius chessmaster and FBI consultant Artemis Blythe swore she'd never return to the misty Cascade Mountains.

Her father—a notorious serial killer, responsible for the deaths of seven women—is now imprisoned, in no small part due to a clue she provided nearly fifteen years ago.And now her father wants his vengeance.

A new serial killer is hunting the wealthy and the elite in the town of Pinelake. Artemis' father claims he knows the identity of the killer, but he'll only tell daughter dearest. Against her will, she finds herself forced back to her old stomping grounds.

Once known as a child chess prodigy, now the locals only think of her as 'The Ghostkiller's' daughter.In the face of a shamed family name and a brother involved with the Seattle mob, Artemis endeavors to use her tactical genius to solve the baffling case.

Hunting a murderer who strikes without a trace, if she fails, the next skeleton in her closet will be her own.

Want to know more?

Greenfield press is the brainchild of bestselling author Steve Higgs. He specializes in writing fast paced adventurous mystery and urban fantasy with a humorous lilt. Having made his money publishing his own work, Steve went looking for a few 'special' authors whose work he believed in.

Georgia Wagner was the first of those, but to find out more and to be the first to hear about new releases and what is coming next, you can join the Facebook group by copying the following link into your browser - www.facebook.com/GreenfieldPress

GREENFIELD PRESS

About the Author

Georgia Wagner worked as a ghost writer for many, many years before finally taking the plunge into self-publishing. Location and character are two big factors for Georgia, and getting those right allows the story to flow seamlessly onto the page. And flow it does, because Georgia is so prolific a new term is required to describe the rate at which nerve-tingling stories find their way into print.

When not found attached to a laptop, Georgia likes spending time in local arboretums, among the trees and ponds. An avid cultivator of orchids, begonias, and all things floral, Georgia also has a strong penchant for art, paintings, and sculptures. A many-decades long passion for mystery novels and years of chess tournament experience makes Georgia the perfect person to pen the Artemis Blythe series.

Printed in Great Britain
by Amazon

42878149R00139